RIGGED FOR MURDER

A Charley Hall Mystery, Book 2

Brenda Gayle

Rigged for Murder
(A Charley Hall Mystery, Book 2)
by Brenda Gayle

Published Internationally by Bowstring Books
Ottawa, Ontario, Canada

EBOOK ISBN 978-1-9990185-7-3
PRINT ISBN 978-1-7775824-2-5

A special thanks to Maddy Mackay and her rowing friends for their inspiring suggestions of titles for this book. Among the runners up were: Rigger Mortis (my personal favourite), Murder on Starboard/Port, Catch a Killer, Murder in the Boathouse, and Kill-Oar. Such a creative bunch.

I hope you enjoy Rigged for Murder.

"SOMEONE JUST FILED a missing person on Alderman Cannon."

Charley Hall's head jerked up and she glared across the newsroom at the man who'd made the pronouncement. It wasn't so much how the word "missing" landed like a punch to the gut that unnerved her as it was the glee in Lester Pyne's voice. He smelled a scoop.

"That's ridiculous," she said, rising from the desk she'd been relegated to. "I spoke to him not very long ago." In her head, she tried to figure out when that had been. Surely it was only a day or two ago. He'd asked her to accompany him to a rowing regatta last weekend. When was that? Last Wednesday? Thursday, maybe? What day was today? Oh, heck. It was Wednesday, again. Had it really been a week? "Who would make such an outrageous claim?"

Pyne's pale face flushed, and he pounded his cigarette butt into the ashtray. The action knocked out several other discarded butts from the overfull bowl. "My contact says it was his secretary. A Miss Diana Huff."

Phew, Charley blew out her annoyance. What the heck was the woman thinking? Dan had probably simply forgotten to update her on his schedule and she, typically, was over-reacting.

"It's a legitimate lead," Pyne added defensively.

"What lead?" the *Kingston Tribune*'s managing editor, John Sherman, said from his doorway.

Shoot! Charley had hoped to nip Pyne's story before he ran with it, but now that Sherman was aware of it, she needed to find another solution. Even if Dan was missing—there was that word again—she needed to keep it out of the newspaper.

"Dan was in St. Catharines for a rowing regatta last weekend. He probably took an extra day or two of vacation and forgot to let his secretary know," Charley said, crossing the room to stand beside her old desk. "If he was missing, why wouldn't his parents have alerted the police?"

"Do we know if he made it to the regatta?" Sherman asked. Pyne shrugged and Sherman expelled an exasperated breath. "Well, find out."

Charley tried not to relish in the panic she saw on Pyne's face. She didn't dislike the man as much as resent him for taking her place as a city reporter. She appreciated that he'd fought for his country—although, truth be told, she found it hard to envision the pudgy, baby-faced mama's boy in a military uniform—but did that mean she had to forfeit all she'd done to build her career as a top-notch reporter just so he'd have a job?

The world had changed while the men had been fighting Hitler and Tojo. Women had stepped up and proven themselves more than capable of making meaningful contributions to society. Surely there was a way for members of both sexes to work in harmony.

She knew Sherman's offer for her to take over the women's pages was meant to be an olive branch. And if it had been any other section of the newspaper, she would have viewed it as a promotion. But going from hard news to fashion and society reporting was a bitter pill to swallow. After all, she wasn't any old reporter. Her grandfather had founded the *Trib* half a century ago but was forced to sell it during the economically turbulent 1930s. Still, the Stormont name was held in high regard by the new publisher—indeed, by everyone in the news business.

After two months, Charley still wasn't completely comfortable with her new role. Although she was doing the work, she'd refused to have her name listed as editor on the masthead, and she'd balked when Sherman had proposed she use her maiden name, Charlotte Stormont. Along with articles about the latest fashions or who had attended what fundraiser, she had managed to slip in stories of more consequence, such as the plight of war widows or destitute mothers. So far, no reader had complained, so Sherman had turned a blind eye.

Nevertheless, she was determined to get her old job back. Pyne wasn't up to the challenge. Sherman would eventually have to acknowledge that. She glanced at her editor, but he wasn't looking at his city reporter for answers. He was staring at her.

Fine! She'd step in and rescue Pyne—again. *Kindness not knives, kindness not knives*, she repeated the mantra her grandmother had drilled into her since childhood. "Martin?" she called to the sports editor whose desk was even further removed than her own from the action of the newsroom. "Did you cover the rowing regatta in St. Catharines over the weekend?"

"Jeez, Charley," Stan Martin said, ambling over to the group, "I thought you read the *Trib* cover-to-cover."

It was a running joke between Charley and Stan that she never read the sports pages and he never read the rest of the paper. Stan had been a mentor to her since she'd first started out as a copy editor, and he'd been almost as incensed as she was over her removal from the city beat.

"Humour me," she replied.

"There was a two-page spread in Monday's edition. The regatta was a big deal because it determined who will represent Canada in rowing at the Olympics next month."

"Did Dan Cannon compete?"

"Sure did. Single sculls. Won his class quite handily, too."

Charley was pleased for Dan. He'd been a lifelong member of the Frontenac Rowing Club and had captained the Queen's University team almost a decade ago. Recently, he'd turned his focus toward the London Olympics as a way to raise his profile before entering federal politics.

She turned back to Sherman. "So, we know where he was this past weekend. I don't think there's a story here."

"There's an official missing person report." Pyne ran his hand over his head, nervously combing the thinning blond strands of hair. "The police are involved."

"Are you sure your source isn't mistaken?" Charley asked, wondering who on the force was feeding Pyne information.

"He's rock solid."

"So, we've got a missing person report filed by Cannon's secretary and police verification," Sherman said. "That's good enough for me. Let's run with it."

"Wait!" Charley glared at the two men. "You can't mention the cop unless you want Pyne's source to dry up. And as for the missing person report, I am not sure Diana Huff is all that reliable. All you're going to be able to write is 'anonymous sources claim a city alderman has gone missing.' That's not good journalism."

"What do you suggest, then?" Pyne's pasty white face turned pink.

Charley turned to Sherman. "I know the family. Let me talk to Dan's parents, see if there's any truth to this." She glanced back at Pyne before continuing. "You know the stature of the Cannons in this city. We don't want to write any half-baked stories that haven't been corroborated."

"You've got a point." Sherman pushed his round spectacles up onto his head and rubbed his eyes.

"But it's my story." Realizing his scoop was about to slip through his hands, Pyne's voice had risen an octave.

"It's not a story at all until it's been substantiated, and Hall is in the best position to do that," Sherman said.

"Think of the reputation of the *Trib*," Charley said, unable to stop the dig. She'd given away several of her own scoops to Pyne in the best interest of the paper. "We're all on the same team, right?"

Pyne sank into his chair, deflated. "I guess so."

"And if you want to give me the name of your contact at Kingston PD..." Charley gave him a saccharine smile. She knew he wouldn't, but she wanted him to refuse in front of their boss.

Sorry, Gran. Sometimes a sharp edge is required.

"Can't do that. I promised him anonymity."

"You confirm the tip, Hall," Sherman said, turning back toward his office. "I'll expect ten inches by deadline."

At least there were no reporters camped out on the Cannons' front lawn. That probably meant Pyne's source hadn't spilled the beans to the *Kingston Whig-Standard*, the *Trib*'s major competitor.

Charley raised her hand to grab the knocker, then let it drop to her side.

Missing?

How could so much anxiety and uncertainty be wrapped up into one small word?

It had to be a mistake. Dan couldn't be missing.

But he wouldn't simply disappear on her, either. He, more than anyone, knew what she'd been through—was still going through. Thoughts about the war and how it had affected her life still rubbed her emotions raw.

She was newly married when her husband, Theo, joined up along with her brother, Freddie, anxious for adventure and the opportunity to see the world. The Dieppe raid in August 1942 changed everything. Letters from Theo and her brother had stopped. After making numerous enquiries Charley was informed by the Canadian authorities that they were missing and presumed dead.

The anguish had been overwhelming. Yet, somehow the world continued as if the two most important men in her life hadn't been taken from her. The sun rose and set as it always had. The streets were as familiar as ever. Charley went to work, did her job and returned home, fully aware that her brother and husband would never return from theirs. Gran had been her rock. But then, Bessie was well acquainted with grief, having already buried her son and husband. Theo's parents, however, were unable to see any path to normalcy without their only child, and moved to another province, cutting all ties with Kingston.

Then, two years ago, almost a year after VE day, Freddie miraculously returned home. He wouldn't talk about what had happened to him over there or where he ended up after the war.

But where was Theo? What had happened to him? If Freddie had come home, why not her husband? Without answers, so much of her life remained unresolved, especially her private life.

Dan wanted her to move on with him, but she couldn't. After all this time, no one would judge her, but she couldn't help feeling she was undeserving. While she'd adored Theo, he was her brother's best friend, and their wedding had been hastily arranged in the pre-war frenzy. Swept up in their enthusiasm, Charley didn't fully realize the consequences until she found herself married to a man she wasn't in love with, a man who was honorably fighting for her country a world away.

They would have made it work if he had come home. But he hadn't. Her husband was and maybe always would be...*missing*.

Charley shook off the melancholy and seized the knocker, rapping it loudly on the door.

This was different. *This* she could do something about.

Hadn't she found Freddie when he'd mysteriously disappeared a few months ago?

The door opened, but rather than the Cannons' usual housekeeper, Rose Cannon herself stood on the threshold. Her blue eyes were red and puffy.

"Oh, Charlotte, thank heavens it's you. Have you spoken with Daniel?" She pulled Charley into the vestibule and quickly closed the door.

"It's true then." Charley's shoulders sagged and her legs felt like lead as she followed Rose into the sitting room. "He's missing."

"We haven't heard from him in days. He was supposed to be back by now." Her head whipped around. "If you haven't heard from him, why are you here?"

"His secretary reported him missing to the police and an informant told one of the reporters in the newsroom."

"Oh, no, no, no." Rose was clearly distraught as she sank down onto the couch. "I had Diana contact the police. We were trying to keep it quiet. We don't want to jeopardize his political career."

"It's pretty tough to keep a lid on things once the police get involved." Charley paced to the window. She wasn't sure how she was going to handle this. Sherman expected a story. She could stall, but not for very long. A missing alderman was a big deal and the *Whig-Standard* was sure to catch wind of it. The only issue was when. She couldn't allow the competition to scoop her, but how far did her loyalty to the *Trib* go?

She watched with dismay as a police car pulled to a stop in the laneway. Constables Marillo and Adams stepped out of the cruiser and headed toward the front door.

Time's up.

"The police are here. I'll let them in."

Charley opened the door just as Constable Marillo was reaching for the knocker. If he was surprised to see her, he gave no indication of it.

"Mrs. Hall." Marillo nodded to her as he and his younger partner entered the house.

"Mrs. Cannon is this way," Charley said, leading them into the sitting room. She made the brief introductions and then stepped back to allow Rose to answer their questions. The constables were thorough, and Charley listened attentively, hoping for some bit of information that could shed some light on what had happened to Dan. There was nothing new. He'd gone to a rowing regatta in St. Catharines last weekend and had been expected to return Sunday night. He hadn't checked in—neither with his family nor his secretary. The officers turned to Charley and she shook her head to say he hadn't contacted her, either.

There'd been no ransom demand. That was good, wasn't it? She was tempted to ask but stopped herself. There was no point in further upsetting Rose by speculating about a possible kidnapping.

Marillo tucked his notepad into his breast pocket and stood. "We have the description of his car. We'll send out a notice to the Ontario Provincial Police as well as the St. Catharines detachment. Don't worry, Mrs. Cannon, I'm sure we'll find him."

"Yeah, he probably went on a bender to celebrate his success at the regatta. I heard he won his class," Adams added.

If looks could kill, Adams would surely be dead. Charley wasn't sure who had the most ferocious glare, Rose or Marillo. The man obviously didn't know Dan at all.

"I am sure there's a perfectly reasonable explanation."

Charley sat down beside Rose and took her hand. "Now that the police are on it, he'll be home in no time."

Rose squeezed Charley's hand as if she was reassured, but her eyes didn't look nearly as confident.

"I'll show you out." Charley stood, anxious to send the constables on their way.

As she watched the men walk toward their cruiser, her eyes widened at the Ford Woody wagon turning into the laneway, a narrow wooden boat tied to its roof.

"Rose!" she yelled. "Come quick. He's home. Dan's home."

Charley raced past the police officers and stopped beside the driver's door to the Woody. It was all she could do not to yank open the door and drag the man from his vehicle. She hopped from foot to foot impatiently waiting while a surprised Dan stepped out of his car. She rushed forward, wrapped her arms around his neck and kissed him fully on the mouth.

She'd never felt so relieved to see anyone in her life.

Then she stepped back and slapped him hard across the cheek.

She'd never felt so angry with anyone in her life.

"CHARLOTTE!" Rose's outrage echoed across the front lawn.

"Well, I guess we're done here," Marillo said opening the door to the police cruiser. "Welcome home, Alderman."

Adams smirked as he got into the car beside his partner. The engine started and the patrol car edged around the Woody and out into the street.

Charley continued to glare at Dan, a small sense of satisfaction breaching her anger as she watched his cheek turn a deep red where she'd struck him.

Dan seemed shocked by her reaction. He glanced between his mother and Charley, confusion clouding his amber-coloured eyes. "What did I do?" He gingerly touched his cheek and winced slightly.

Charley turned away and started to head down the laneway, away from the house.

"Oh, no you don't." Dan grabbed her arm. "You don't get to kiss me like that and then slug me without an explanation."

"Ask your mother."

"Both of you. Inside. Now!"

Rose's tone didn't countenance any argument and,

feeling like a naughty child about to face a serious reprimand, Charley followed Dan into the house. She saw Rose stiffen as Dan bent to give her a kiss on the cheek. Dan would be lucky if his only punishment was the wallop Charley had given him.

Rose directed them into the sitting room and pointed to the couch. Sitting beside Dan, Charley started to wonder if perhaps she had overreacted a tad. Her hand stung from the impact of the slap. She glanced up at him. He was going to have a serious bruise. That would be fun to try to explain to people.

Rose took the seat across from them. She folded her hands neatly on her lap and took a deep breath. "Where have you been, Daniel?" Her voice was calm, almost devoid of emotion.

"What do you mean? I was at the rowing regatta."

"The regatta ended three days ago," Charley interjected.

"Charlotte, please. Let me handle this."

Even though Rose hadn't raised her voice, Charley felt as if she'd been soundly chastised. She leaned back and bit the inside of her cheek to stop herself from making any further comments.

"Yeah, I know the regatta ended a few days ago. And I meant to come home, but..." Dan leapt to his feet and started pacing the room. "Things didn't go so well."

"But you won." Charley, unable to keep silent, glanced guiltily at Rose. When the older woman didn't censure her, she continued. "And quite handily, I'm told."

"Yes, I won. And that should have meant I'd qualified to go to London as part of the Canadian Olympic Team."

"But you didn't?" Charley wasn't a sports fan, but it seemed to her if someone won their class at an Olympic trial that should qualify them for the big event. "Why not?"

"Good question," Dan replied bitterly. "I'll give you two words: Frank Beanish."

"Frank Beanish?" Rose said. "My goodness, what on earth does Frank have to do with it?"

"Who is Frank Beanish?" Charley didn't recognize the name, but apparently Rose did. And it was significant to Dan, too, given the venom of his tone.

"Well, currently he is in charge of determining who goes to London to row for Canada. But about ten years ago, he was the coach of Queen's University's rowing team."

"Oh, no." Charley closed her eyes. She remembered the incident very well. As a hazing prank, senior members of the rowing team had loosened the rigging for the oars on a rookie's scull and drilled tiny holes into the stern. As a result, the novice rower had found himself trapped in a sinking boat in the middle of the St. Lawrence River, unable to manipulate his way back to shore. The rower survived but quit the team. Dan had tried to get the culprits punished, but the coach refused to take action, claiming it was all part of the process to separate the wheat from the chaff. Not willing to give up, Dan took his complaint right up to the university principal and the next season, the team had a new coach. "Beanish was the coach you had fired."

"It's not *me*, specifically, you understand," Dan said in a way that told her that despite his words, he fully believed Beanish had a vendetta against him. "The committee has determined it will only send a doubles team and a men's eight."

"Can they do that? Block you from competing?" Rose asked.

Dan shrugged. "They can do whatever they want. My

time was excellent—well, better than the qualifying minimum. I'm convinced it would have put me in medal contention. I tried arguing with the committee but to no avail. I'm certain Beanish blackballed me as payback."

"Is there someone you can appeal to? A higher authority?" Charley asked.

"No, the sport committees make their own decisions."

"Well, that's very unfortunate," Rose said, "but it hardly explains where you've been for the past three days."

"Yeah, sorry about that. I was so mad when they told me I wasn't going to London, I took off. There was another regatta being held in Philadelphia. I thought, maybe if I won that one, beat the top American sculler, they'd have to reconsider."

"I take it you didn't win," Charley said.

Dan shrugged. "I might have, but I was too late arriving. They wouldn't let me enter the competition. So, I hung around and watched for a few days and then made my way back here."

"You didn't think to call and let anyone know where you were?" Rose asked.

"Sorry, Mother, my head wasn't on straight."

"I should say it wasn't. You gave us all quite a fright."

"Not to mention, you almost became the *Trib*'s headline story," Charley added.

Rose frowned. "You aren't going to write anything, are you?"

"Well, I am going to have to write *something*. But don't worry, it will be so innocuous, it will be relegated to the back of the paper somewhere." For the first time she could remember, Charley wasn't anxious to get her story on page one. She stood up. "And with that in mind, I'd better get to it. My editor will be screaming blue murder if I don't get him his ten inches by deadline."

"I'll walk you out," Dan said.

"You won't forget about tomorrow, will you?" Rose called after her.

"Tomorrow?"

"You and your grandmother are pouring at the Frontenac Rowing Club, for the Dominion Day tea."

"We are?" Charley was certain this was the first she'd heard of it. She threw Dan a questioning glance. He shrugged.

"It's been planned for weeks," Rose pressed. "We always have a big do July first. And this year will be extra special because the president is retiring."

Charley was sure she heard Dan mutter "finally" under his breath.

"All right, then, I guess I'll see you tomorrow," Charley said, cursing her grandmother for committing her to yet another society function.

Dan reached over Charley's shoulder to stop her from opening the front door. "Maybe after the tea, you and I could watch the fireworks together," he suggested.

"I don't know if I've forgiven you yet." She crossed her arms over her chest.

Dan's eyes crinkled at the corners as he grinned down at her.

Darn, why did he have to look at her like that? She felt a flush creep up from her neck to her cheeks as he stepped closer, almost pinning her against the door.

"It's nice to know you missed me," he said softly.

Charley put a hand to his chest. "Come any closer and I'll give you a matching bruise on your other cheek."

"Do I get the kiss first? It would be worth it."

"You're impossible!" She reached behind her back for the handle, pulled the door inward, and executed what she thought was a lovely pirouette to make her escape.

"I'll see you tomorrow," he called after her as she jogged down the steps.

Her heart hammered in her chest. *Damn him.* She was looking forward to it more than she cared to admit.

Charley peeled back the elbow-length white gloves, now stained with tea and jam, and threw them on the hall stand. Then she tackled the wine-coloured, velour cocktail hat, stabbing it with its pin before tossing it on top of the gloves. She reached up to release her hair from the uncomfortable victory roll coiffure Gran had insisted she wear.

"You're back."

Charley glanced up as Freddie, dressed comfortably in a pair of wide-leg, light grey trousers and knitted, short-sleeved, red-and-white-striped shirt, descended the stairs. It wasn't fair that men could dress for comfort while women were supposed to dress for exhibition. He looked freshly showered; his damp, red hair slightly curling at the ends, and a few droplets of water still clinging to his beard.

"Your powers of observation are stellar, as usual" she replied, raking her fingers along her aching scalp as she loosened her shoulder-length chestnut brown hair.

"You're in a mood." Freddie paused on the bottom step. "Dare I approach?"

"Sorry." Charley grimaced. She *was* in a mood, but it wasn't her brother's fault. "I can't wait to get out of this dress and back into my normal clothes. That tea was so boring." *And pretentious*, but she kept that comment to herself.

"What did you do with Gran?"

"She's still outside talking with Mr. Arcadi, our cabbie." Charley didn't like it. Romeo Arcadi had taken it upon himself to become her personal driver. She wasn't sure how he did it, but every time she called for a cab, Romeo was the one who showed up—day or night. He wasn't supposed to drive them home today, but when Dan had disappeared from the tea, she had no choice. And now Gran knew about Arcadi and was pestering him for information about Charley's travel habits.

"Such a nice man," Gran said, entering the hallway. "It makes me feel better to know he's looking out for you."

"He's not 'looking out for me'," Charley said. "He just drives me sometimes. When I'm on a story."

"But the places you go..."

Gran left the sentence unfinished and Charley hoped that would be the end of it. But Freddie dashed that thought.

"Should I meet this fellow? Are his intentions honorable?"

"Oh, for heaven's sake! He's old enough to be our father," Charley snapped. "All I know is when I need a cab, he's there."

"Okay, okay, keep your hat on—well not literally, of course." Freddie's eyes crinkled with humour and his lips twitched behind his too-bushy, red beard. "As your big brother, I'm simply fulfilling my fraternal responsibility to ensure your well-being."

The irony wasn't lost on Charley. Since he'd returned from the war, Freddie could barely take care of himself, let alone anyone else. Charley didn't bother snapping back a retort. She'd begun keeping to herself her thoughts about all the men in her life thinking she needed looking after.

"How was the tea, Gran?" Freddie turned his attention to their grandmother.

Bessie Stormont was executing a much more placid removal of her gloves and pillbox hat. "It was quite nice," she replied. "The speech by Robin Carter was a bit tedious, however. How that man loves to hear himself talk. I thought he might have censored himself, though, given how late he was in taking the podium. So inconsiderate to the organizers. How he managed to be elected president of the rowing club for so many years is a mystery."

"I didn't get the impression he was going willingly," Charley said.

"Well, after twenty-five years it is definitely time for fresh blood."

"It's been that long?"

"Oh, yes. I remember it clearly. He was elected the same summer as the accident."

The accident—the one where her parents drowned. "Why would you associate those two things?"

"Well, why wouldn't I? Your father was a prominent member of the Frontenac Rowing Club."

"He was? I didn't know that." She turned to Freddie. "Did you know that?"

Freddie shrugged. "Sure. I thought you knew. Grandpa was a founder of the club and our father was pretty successful, too. Rowing was like a family legacy—until me, at least."

"I knew he was a sailor, but..."

"Your father loved anything that travelled on the water," Gran said. "There are pictures of him at the club...I never thought to point them out to you... You should look for them next time you're there." She glanced around. "Now, where is that housekeeper? I'd like a bit of sherry before dinner to wash down all that tea."

"You gave her the afternoon and evening off to celebrate Dominion Day," Charley said.

"Did I?" Gran raised an eyebrow, completely aware she had done no such thing. "How generous of me. Well, I shall have to muddle through on my own, then."

Charley watched Gran enter the salon and then turned to Freddie. "I think this housekeeper might last a little longer than the last one; I'm giving her a full six months."

The latest housekeeper was older and more seasoned than the previous one. Charley had really liked Chantal, the tiny, young French girl her grandmother had hired earlier in the spring. But Chantal had had a tough time keeping up with the formidable Bessie Stormont; she handed in her notice after a month, as Charley had predicted. It remained to be seen how Irena would fare.

"You're dreaming. Six weeks. Less if she thinks she can come to you to get leave rather than going to Gran."

"Well, it *is* a holiday," Charley said. "And Gran can seem a bit intimidating until you get to know her."

"And even then." Freddie laughed.

"Are you ready to go? It'll only take me a minute to change. You can go get the picnic hamper Irena made up before she left." Charley had been looking forward to spending what remained of the afternoon and evening in the park by the water. There would be music and games and, of course, fireworks.

"No can do. I only came home to change. Our baseball game was rained out and we were all soaked to the skin. That was quite the storm, but I heard it was fairly isolated. My mate, up a ways on Division Street, said it barely wet the pavement. What about at the waterfront?"

"It came out of nowhere." Charley shivered remembering how quickly the skies had darkened and the torrential downpour that followed. "The Royal Canadian Mounted Police even had to come rescue a couple of inexperienced boaters who became stranded on the lake. Strange, isn't it? Picturing Mounties on the water? But I guess Lake Ontario falls under federal jurisdiction."

"Strange days indeed," Freddie agreed. "Well, I'm off to Beaup's with some of the lads."

Charley's heart sank. *Beaupré's Tavern.* She had hoped when she found her brother suffering from hallucinations and the painful physical effects of alcohol withdrawal two months ago, that he'd been serious about wanting to get sober. But almost immediately after regaining his senses, he'd returned to drinking. She knew it had to do with his time as a POW in the war and all he had seen and done—but never talked about—and it pained her that she was unable to help him.

How much of it had to do with Theo? Charley had raised the issue with Freddie a few times, but each time he'd spiraled into a deeper, darker state of despair to the point that she'd stopped asking.

"Don't wait up," Freddie said as he grabbed his hat from the coat rack, kissed her on the cheek and headed out.

After hanging up her dress and slipping into a pair of wide, pleated pants and a sailor blouse, Charley collapsed onto her bed. Who knew pouring tea could be so exhausting? Or maybe it was the fact that all her plans for the day had gone haywire.

She sat up.

Enough feeling sorry for yourself.

Just because she had no one to go to the picnic with

didn't mean she shouldn't go. The whole town was going to be there. She was bound to run into people she knew.

The private telephone Gran had insisted she install in her room sounded. She glanced at her watch. Surely Sherman wasn't calling with a story for her this late in the afternoon. There was no *Tribune* today, and what could be so important on the women's pages that it had to be dealt with on a holiday?

The telephone rang three more times. She was sorely tempted to ignore it, just to annoy her editor, but then curiosity got the better of her. What else did she have to do today?

"Hello?"

"Charley, thank goodness you're there."

"Dan? Where the heck have you been? You were sup—"

"Wait! Stop talking. This is important. I need your help."

Tendrils of fear snaked up from Charley's heart and wrapped around her throat so she couldn't speak. The few seconds that elapsed before he continued seemed like an eternity.

"I'm at the police station. I've been arrested..."

"WHERE IS EVERYONE?" Charley stood in the entrance of the police station. She had never witnessed it so eerily quiet.

"Give it time," Constable Marillo said, ambling out of the Sergeant's Office to her right. "I expect a full house tonight." He approached Charley. "I'm a bit surprised he called you, Mrs. Hall. I would have thought he'd want to speak with a lawyer."

Charley shrugged. She didn't know what was going on —her brain seemed to stop working after Dan exclaimed he'd been arrested for murder.

Murder?

She'd tried to sort it out as she'd walked to the station: walking helped her make sense from what at first seemed incomprehensible. It usually worked when she was investigating a story for the *Trib*. But not tonight.

"What's going on? Why is Dan here?" Another thought occurred to her and she cocked her head. "Why are *you* here?"

"Why wouldn't I be here? A prominent member of the community has been arrested for murder. That's not the type of supervision you hand over to a rookie." His voice was monotone as if he was simply repeating the words by rote. Then he shrugged. "Bureaucracy."

Charley leaned back against the wall and stared into the face of the senior officer. He had to be in his fifties and yet he remained a constable. In the five years she'd been working the city beat, she'd seen him train three younger men, only to watch them pass him on their way up the police hierarchy's ladder. "Why do you put up with it?"

She watched as confusion crossed his face and was about to explain her question when his mouth twisted into a bitter grin. "Why do you?"

Now it was her turn to be confused. "I don't know what you mean."

He snorted. "Sure you do. I read the *Trib* every day. You don't think I've noticed that you're no longer on the city beat? You may not be signing your name, but I know you're writing for the women's pages now." He crossed his arms over his chest and leaned against a filing cabinet. "My wife loves that, by the way. And I have to agree—for the first time in my life I'm actually reading them. But your replacement, what's his name? Pyne? A complete hack. I don't know why the folks in charge don't realize it, but they never do..."

Charley gaped at the constable, speechless at his sudden candor. In the next moment, his demeanour changed, and he snapped to attention. A mask of impersonality descended over his face, and he appeared to loom larger in the police station's lobby. He motioned towards the Sergeant's Office. "You can wait in there. I'll bring him to you." He turned on his heel, unlocked a door, and headed down the corridor that led to the cell blocks.

Charley wandered into the office and sat down on one of the chairs in front of the desk as she tried to process what had just happened. She had no idea anyone else felt that way about the inequalities of the workplace. Marillo knew—no, not knew—he shared her frustration. She felt a surprising glow of kinship towards the usually taciturn constable and then chastised herself for such fanciful thoughts. Still, it was nice to know someone had noticed the decline in reporting on the city beat.

She glanced up at the sound of metal dragging along the corridor.

Surely not!

But there he was, chained hands and feet, shuffling into the office. Her heart lurched and she leapt from the chair. "Is this really necessary?" she asked, pointing to the offending shackles.

"He's charged with murder," Marillo said. "I'm not even supposed to let you see him."

"It's fine, Charley. Constable Marillo is only doing his job." Dan had used his conciliatory politician's tone, which told Charley it was definitely not fine, but he didn't want her to make an issue of it.

"Only a few minutes," Marillo said. Then pausing on the threshold, he added, "And no physical contact." He stepped out of the room but kept the door ajar.

"He's right, you know," Dan said. "This is definitely against the rules."

She slumped into the chair and watched Dan adjusting the chain that ran from his arms, around his body to his feet before taking the chair beside her. He wore someone else's clothes—someone considerably smaller than his six-foot, broad-chested frame. The brown pants were too short while the tan-coloured shirt stretched tightly across his chest, and the sleeves wouldn't extend all the way to his wrists. No socks. No shoes. No belt. No tie.

"Thank you for coming," he said.

"What's going on, Dan? Murder? Who? How?"

"Frank Beanish." He raised his hands to his face. She

tried to ignore the jangling of the chains. "I didn't do it. They haven't even told me how he was killed."

Charley's heart broke that he thought he'd have to profess his innocence to her, of all people. "Of course, you didn't," she said vehemently. Her mind was whirling with possibilities. It was a mistake. It had to be. "Why did they arrest you? Is it because you had an argument with him about the Olympic team? That's not enough evidence."

Dan raised his head. He looked pale and...scared. "I was there. They found me with him. But I swear, Charley, he was dead when I arrived. I was about to call the police when..."

His voice had risen in pitch and his breathing was coming in short bursts. Charley recognized he was starting to become hysterical. She squatted beside him and wrapped her arms around him for comfort.

No physical contact be damned!

Dan relaxed into her and rested his head against hers. She could feel his breathing return to normal. Then he sat up straighter and pulled away from her. "I'm okay," he said. "Thanks."

She kept hold of his hands and hooked her foot around the leg of her chair to bring it closer to his. She sat down but wouldn't let go of him. She didn't know which of them needed the comfort of touch more.

"Why don't you start at the beginning. You went to see Beanish? Why?"

He nodded. "My secretary got a message that he wanted to see me. Today. This afternoon. I thought maybe the Olympic Committee had changed its mind."

"When did you get the message? You never said anything to me about it when I saw you at the rowing club."

"It was shortly after you arrived. I was going to tell you,

but you were so busy pouring tea..." He gave her an apologetic smile. "I thought since he lives right across the river from the club—he was renting the old Foster house—I could take one of the sculls, go see him and be back well before anyone missed me. Besides, I was more than happy for an excuse to miss out on Robin Carter's farewell accolade to himself."

"I wish I'd been so fortunate," Charley murmured. "So, what happened when you got there?"

"I tied up my scull to the dock and went up to the house. I knocked but no one answered. I started to get a bit peeved. I mean, what was Beanish playing at? I headed back down to the waterfront and noticed that the door to the boathouse was open. I called out, thinking he must be in there, but there was no answer."

The back of Charley's neck prickled from anticipation. She dreaded what was coming next. "You went inside?"

"Well sure. I mean, I'd gone there to talk to the man, I wanted to find him."

"And you did. Dead."

Dan's face took on a greenish pallor as he recalled to her what he'd seen. "It was dim in the boathouse, but I could see him—well, a body anyway. I assumed it was Beanish. There was an awful smell. And flies everywhere." He seemed to stifle a gag on the words. "I called his name, but the body didn't move. So, I went closer. I didn't know if he was dead, injured, or sleeping it off, you understand?"

Charley nodded. She understood all too well. It was only a few months ago she'd stumbled across a body and had responded the same way—forcing herself to look closer, to be certain. But the police—Marillo—had believed her when she'd called them, told them what she'd found.

"Did you touch anything?" she asked.

"As I said, it was dark, hard to see. There was something sticky on the floor and when I got closer to him, I slipped, lost my footing..."

Charley closed her eyes and whispered a small prayer to protect him.

"I fell and my hands were sticky. I wiped them on my clothes. I scrambled to my feet and was running to the door. I was going to call the police. Truly Charley, I was."

He was starting to panic again. She squeezed his hands to let him know she believed him.

"When I got out of the boathouse, the police were already there. I tried to explain, to tell them what had happened, but they wouldn't listen to me. That's when I realized it was blood. The sticky stuff. I was covered in Beanish's blood! They arrested me and brought me here."

Charley could hear a commotion outside the office door and knew they didn't have much longer. The rowdiest of the Dominion Day celebrants were about to be brought in to sleep off their drunkenness. "What can I do?" she asked.

"You have to help me."

"I'm not a lawyer," she said.

"I'm a lawyer—" Dan began and held up his hand to stop her from interrupting him. "I know, not a criminal lawyer, but I did have to study the law for murder when I took my exams. I know what a lawyer can and cannot do in this situation." He looked earnestly into her eyes. "The police figure they have their man so they're not going to do anything more. I need you, Charley. I need your investigation skills to find out what really happened to Frank Beanish."

Charley and Dan quickly disengaged their hands as Marillo walked into the room. "Time's up. I'm sorry."

To give him credit, Charley thought the constable

seemed sincerely sorry to have to interrupt them. "What's going to happen to him?"

"He'll go back to the cells for tonight. Likely before a judge tomorrow."

"But he will be released on bail, right?"

Marillo shrugged. "Hard to say. It's a murder charge and he's got money and resources. The court may see him as a flight risk."

"I wouldn't!" Dan said.

Marillo looked unimpressed. "Like I said, hard to say."

"But all you've got is his presence at the scene of the crime," Charley pushed. "He told you Beanish was already dead when he arrived. You've no proof otherwise."

"I can't speak to the evidence. It will likely all come out tomorrow." Marillo took Dan's elbow and urged him to his feet.

"I'll be fine," Dan said to Charley. "Call my mother and tell her what's going on. She'll arrange for a lawyer." He shuffled toward the door. "And the other thing..."

"I'll do what I can," Charley said. "Constable, can I use your phone?"

"But be quick about it. This place is about to get very busy."

Charley eased the door closed behind them. She didn't want anyone overhearing this conversation. She opened her pocketbook and withdrew the small business card that had arrived at her house several weeks ago. It said: "Call anytime, day or night."

She glanced at the clock on the wall—seven-forty-five on a holiday evening—and hoped that was true.

6

Bail was denied.

It was inconceivable to Charley that a prominent member of society was being treated no better than a criminal. Dan had been characterized as a spoiled and privileged dandy used to getting his own way. She wasn't sure how the Crown prosecutor had amassed so much history in such a short period of time—literally hours—but he had brought up not only the argument Dan had had with Frank Beanish over his failure to be named to the Olympic rowing team but also Dan's role in having Beanish fired as rowing coach at Queen's over the hazing incident ten years ago. He painted a picture of an angry, bitter man intent on revenge and, perhaps more importantly, with the financial resources to escape justice by leaving the country.

At least she had learned how Beanish died. He'd been attacked with a rowing oar, severely beaten, and succumbed to massive head injuries. All of which played into the prosecutor's theory of motive.

Charley was frustrated with Dan's lawyer, a supposed hotshot criminal specialist he'd known in law school. He'd barely said a word—hadn't even objected when the prosecutor was tarnishing Dan's character with hearsay stories about old grudges.

For his part, Dan, dressed in a freshly pressed blue suit and tie, seemed to take everything in stride. He appeared calm—hardly the wild-eyed killer the Crown attorney was making him out to be—and only uttered the words "not guilty" when asked for a plea from the judge.

Of course, the press loved it all. Holding tightly to Rose's hand, Charley had led her through the throng of reporters—all of whom she knew—to the front of the courtroom and then back out when it was over. She'd always hated this part of the city beat—the feeding frenzy that seemed to occur when someone of note got themselves into a pickle. She preferred a quieter, one-on-one approach to get the real story. However, given what had happened in the courtroom today, there was little chance the real story was going to appear in the various broadsheets any time soon.

"Hey, Hall, how about a scoop?" Lester Pyne saddled up to her after she closed the door to Rose's hired car. It was a bad time for Dan's father to be away, but several of Rose's friends had arrived and promised to stay with her to help her through "this trying period."

"No comment," Charley replied, turning her back on Pyne and the stench of cigarette smoke he brought with him everywhere he went.

"C'mon, do a pal a favour, would ya? It's for the *Trib.*" He trailed her down the street. She could hear several other footsteps join her adversary's, but she didn't turn around.

In front of her, a familiar black taxi eased itself next to the curb and Romeo Arcadi stuck his head out of the window. "Need a lift?"

She slipped into the backseat. "You're a lifesaver."

He chuckled and forced the cab back into traffic, effectively stymieing the pack of reporters chasing her. "Where to?"

She gave him the address, leaned back against the cool leather seat, and closed her eyes. At some point, she'd try to figure out why Arcadi always seemed to be around when she needed him, but for today, she was simply going to thank her lucky stars and leave it at that.

She heard his "tsk-tsk" of displeasure as the taxi drew to a stop outside the old storefront.

"Now, what's wrong with this building?" Charley asked. She glanced out her window. Granted, the neighbourhood had seen better days, but the street still boasted a good collection of retailers and eateries.

Arcadi exited the cab and came around to her side to help her out. "Would you like me to wait for you, ma'am?"

He hadn't answered her question, but she didn't press. "No, thank you. The person I am meeting will have a vehicle."

She followed his gaze to read the freshly painted name on the glass of the front door: Mark Spadina, Private Detective.

"Very well," he replied in a tone she wasn't sure indicated he was satisfied or simply resigned. He didn't drive away until she had opened the door, stepped over the threshold, and turned to wave that she was all right.

"Mrs. Hall!"

She jumped and whirled around. "You shouldn't sneak up on people like that. It's not polite."

"How am I sneaking up on you? It's my office. I assume you're here to see me."

Charley scowled at Mark's back as he led her into a large room off the entryway and motioned for her to take a seat. He liked to unnerve her. She hadn't missed that about him.

Charley took a few moments to reacquaint herself with

Mark as he rounded the large oak desk and descended into his chair. It had been about two months since she'd last seen him. It was her brother's birthday party and he had told her he wasn't planning on immediately returning to his job as a detective with the Toronto Police Department. Overall, he looked the same today as he had then: somewhat dishevelled but not unkempt. His black hair was slightly too long, his face was in need of a shave, and his nose was awkwardly angled. It was his eyes that always got to her: so dark they often appeared black under his heavy dark eyebrows, and capable of regarding her with such piercing intensity that she felt as if she was his prey. Until he smiled—which he didn't do all that often and he wasn't doing now—and then all menace was removed.

"I thought you might have been out. Investigating," she said.

"And yet you came here anyway."

"I just came from the courthouse," she said, choosing to ignore his taunt.

"How did it go?"

"I don't want to talk about it."

Mark shrugged. "Okay. Let me tell you what I've found out." He glanced down at a notepad on his desk. "Your boy and the vic have quite the checkered past together."

"He's not 'my boy'," Charley interrupted him. "He's my friend. And if you want to get picky about it, he's closer to you than he is to me." She saw the jab did its job as Mark winced at the reminder. Dan didn't know it, but he and Mark had the same birth mother. Investigating her death was what had brought Mark to Kingston.

"Fine, your 'friend' has a not-so-friendly past with Mr. Beanish."

"Yes, I'm aware of all that. And all of Kingston will be

aware of it before the day is done since it was brought up in court this morning." Sometimes she hated her profession. "That doesn't mean he killed him."

"No, but it does go to motive."

"Now you're sounding like that prosecutor. Whose side are you on?"

"I work for you, Mrs. Hall. I'm on your side, of course."

"Well, you're not acting like it. You almost seem pleased that Dan's in this predicament."

"I can't claim that I am not taking some small measure of satisfaction in the good alderman being brought down a peg or two. But I promise you, Charley, if he didn't do it, I will find who did."

At least he was honest about his feelings. Although they were half-brothers, their experiences couldn't have been any more different. Mark had been abandoned at birth and raised in an orphanage. He'd worked hard to get everything he had, modest as it was. He thought Dan had been born with a silver spoon in his mouth, and Charley couldn't argue with that. Dan had everything Mark had been denied: two loving parents with means, a good, stable home, and a clear path for his future. Of course, Mark resented him. She wouldn't trust him if he pretended he felt otherwise.

"What else have you found?" Charley asked.

"Well, if we assume Dan Cannon didn't do it—"

"He didn't!"

"As I said..." Mark gave her a patient smile. "I did some checking into the victim's past to see if we could find another suspect." He glanced down and read from his notes. "After he was fired from Queen's University, he left for England. Kept involved with rowing. Was a member of the Twickenham Rowing Club. He worked as a locomotive fireman and then driver out of Feltham and lived in a railway house along the line. When the war broke out, he was considered part of essential services and kept his job rather than being recruited for the war effort."

There was something in Mark's tone that caught Charley's ear. He sounded critical, but surely Mark understood why some professions were deemed essential—hadn't cops been one of them? And Beanish wasn't a young man. He'd fought in the Great War. Certainly one war was enough for anyone. "According to what they said in court this morning, he was fifty-six," Charley said.

"In 1946 he married a young war widow, a Georgia Willig, age thirty—Hmmm," he glanced up, "not much older than you. They moved back to Kingston about six months ago. He seems to have spent most of his time since he got back coaching for the Frontenac Rowing Club. I can't find any real employment."

"I doubt coaching would provide a livable income," Charley said.

"Agreed. I'm concerned about two things. First, his young wife. Not that it's unusual for a man to seek a younger wife, but what did he have to offer her?"

"That says a lot about your attitude toward marriage," Charley said. "You think we're all gold diggers?"

Mark eyed her critically. "Which brings me to my second concern. Why wasn't he employed? Did he suddenly inherit money? Marry for it?"

"You suspect his wife?" Charley's reporter brain was seeking connections.

Mark shrugged. "I always suspect the wife—or husband, whatever the case may be. Did they say where Mrs. Beanish was at the time of the murder when you were in court today?"

Charley shook her head. "No, she wasn't there, and they

only mentioned that he had a wife when they were trying to gain sympathy for the victim at Dan's expense."

"It's not that unusual. I'd have been more surprised if she had shown up for a bail hearing. She won't take my telephone calls and when I tried to go see her earlier today, the coppers wouldn't let me near the place."

"No professional courtesy for a former police officer?"

"My dear Mrs. Hall, don't you know that private detectives are the bane of a police officer's existence? As far as they're concerned, I'm no better than the criminals they're trying to catch."

"Well, that's too bad. I was hoping you could use your connections to convince the police to look for a suspect other than Dan."

"Don't hold your breath. They figure they've got their man. Their job is done."

"Are you saying we're at a dead end?" Charley fought against the hopelessness that was threatening to overwhelm her. "Because I don't think so. There are still avenues we can pursue."

"Absolutely. First thing is to determine whether the new Mrs. Beanish could have been involved in her husband's death."

"But you said she won't speak to you."

Mark's whole countenance changed when he gave her a dazzling smile that exposed blindingly white and perfectly aligned teeth. A rush of heat flooded her face as those piercing black eyes softened to dark chocolate, and she felt their relationship shift from the prickly predator-versus-prey she was accustomed to, to one of co-conspirators. "There's more than one way to skin a cat. Let's go visit an old friend of ours."

Mark held open the door and allowed Charley to precede him through the doors of Richardson Laboratory. Housing the Queen's University pathology department and conveniently situated next to Kingston General Hospital, it was a building she was very familiar with. But she hadn't been here in several months—not since she'd come to confront a murderer and very nearly lost her own life. If Mark hadn't arrived... Well, she didn't want to think about that.

She shook off the ghosts and followed him along the hallway, halting on the threshold of a student lounge.

"Laine!" she said, genuinely pleased to see the young medical intern despite the new ghosts she raised. It seemed there was no way Charley was going to be allowed to forget the drama of two months ago that had begun with a frantic search for her missing brother and led to a murder investigation. She glanced at Mark. Maybe it wasn't such a surprise. It was what had brought the detective to Kingston, too.

"Charley, it's great to see you again," Laine said. "And you, too, Detective." She waved them into the room, then closed and locked the door. "There, now we won't be interrupted."

As she walked past them to a threadbare sofa, Charley

was struck, again, by how tiny she was, probably not even five feet. At five-foot-seven, Charley felt gargantuan next to her.

Laine tucked her feet under herself and smiled expectantly. Her light blue eyes and fair skin were a striking contrast to her dark hair, which she wore very short. If she hadn't seen Laine in action, Charley would have questioned whether the physician-in-training had the moxie to excel in her profession, particularly since female students were few, having only been granted permission by Queen's to study medicine five years earlier, in 1943.

"How is Freddie?" Laine asked, perhaps feeling some of the same ghosts.

Charley sighed and sat across from her. "I wish I could say he was better, that he'd learned his lesson after his brush with death, but he's very much the same."

"I am so sorry to hear that."

Charley shrugged. "At least he hasn't gone on any real benders lately. And he's home before dawn most nights."

Laine nodded. "Poor man. I can't imagine the demons he's trying to keep at bay."

"He won't talk about it—none of it. All we know is that he was at Dieppe, but after that..." Charley shook her head and paused to control the frustration she felt mounting. "We assume he was captured and taken to a German POW camp, but at the time, while he was MIA, we'd heard nothing from him or about him after that horrible battle. We thought he was dead until he suddenly returned home. Where was he during the war? Where was he after the war?" *What happened to Theo?* Charley kept the last, most significant, question to herself.

"We have a floor of vets in the hospital," Laine said in a

somber tone. "Most won't talk about their experiences, either. It's all too awful to comprehend. You're lucky, in so many ways, that at least Freddie is home with you. He is struggling, but he's doing the best he can every day."

"I want my brother back," Charley said. "I know it's selfish. I feel so helpless right now. I don't know what I can do for him."

"You can't make him better, Charley. He must do it his own way, in his own time. All you can do is be there for him. Support him. And maybe, someday, he'll be ready to face whatever happened to him. Maybe, someday, he'll be willing to share."

Charley blinked away the tears. "Do you really think so?"

Laine shrugged. "I can't make any promises. But don't discount the importance of your love and support."

"And the drinking?"

Laine cocked her head to the side and shrugged. "Maybe it's the lesser of two evils. If it's helping him cope, it's better than the alternative."

Laine didn't have to elaborate. Charley had heard enough stories of veterans who had taken their own lives because they were unable to reconcile their wartime experiences with their homecoming.

"I'm sure you're right," Charley said, exhaling a long breath to expel the ghosts in the room.

"Right. Do you have any information for us, Doc?"

Charley jumped at the masculine voice. She'd completely forgotten Mark was with them. He'd remained standing near the door as if it needed to be guarded despite the fact Laine had made a point of locking it.

"Sure do." She turned to Charley. "Detective Spadina

called me last night to see if there was any way I'd be able to... how'd you put it?" She flashed Mark a wicked grin. "... 'get in on the autopsy action.' Well, fortunately for you, all of us fifth years were allowed to watch this morning. It's not often Kingston has a really brutal murder, thank heavens for society's benefit, of course, but for us students, a murder is like pennies from heaven."

"What were the results?" Charley asked.

"Well, the official report will be going to Kingston PD, of course, but the chief pathologist took great delight in making sure all of us got a close-up look at the wounds. I think he was hoping to see me and the one other woman in the room swoon, but it was a couple of the lads who took a tumble, instead." Laine chuckled then quickly sobered. "It was pretty awful, though. The head was where most of the damage had been done, and quite frankly, if you hadn't known who the victim was, you'd never be able to tell from looking at him."

"That bad?" Charley felt some sympathy for the poor physicians who'd fainted as her stomach began to churn at simply hearing Laine's description.

"Yes, it was a very violent attack."

"Weapon?" Mark asked.

"We think it was a wooden oar."

"Do the police have it?"

"Yes, they brought it to see if they could compare it to some of the wounds."

"Do they know where the oar came from?" Charley asked.

Laine shook her head. "If they do, they didn't tell us."

Charley tried to suppress her disappointment. She'd been hoping for more clarity. She was worried the police were going to try to prove the oar came from the boat Dan had arrived in. But Beanish was killed in a boathouse and he was a rower; certainly, there must have been many oars stored there.

A crime of opportunity, rather than pre-meditated?

She glanced at Mark. Was he thinking the same thing?

"Time of death?" he asked.

"That's difficult to say," Laine said. "The boathouse was cool and damp. So that could affect *algor mortis*—the rate the body cools—and *rigor mortis*, the stiffening. All I can say is that it was some time yesterday."

"But *rigor mortis* usually sets in three or more hours after death, right? If he was already stiff when the police arrived—" Charley began.

"Yes, that's true. I know what you're looking for, Charley, but I'm not sure I can help you," Laine said. "There are too many variables that can interfere with the onset and duration of *rigor mortis*. For example, if the victim had been killed during a long, protracted fight or had undergone extreme physical exertion before dying, *rigor mortis* can set in earlier, whereas extensive *antemortem* bleeding—that's bleeding before death—can delay it. And both those situations seem to be present in this case."

"Plus, we only have Alderman Cannon's statement that he'd just found Beanish when the police arrived," Mark added. "He could have killed him earlier in the day and come back—or stayed around."

"Again, I ask you, Detective, whose side are you on?" Charley snapped.

"And again, I tell you, Mrs. Hall, I'm on your side." Mark flashed her a smile. "I know how a cop's mind works, which, I believe, is why you hired me. To stay one step ahead of the police."

Charley sagged. "So, what do we do now?"

"You saw the oar, Doc. How big and heavy would you say it was?"

"About ten feet long. I didn't lift it, but it's solid wood so I would imagine it's pretty darn heavy."

"And unwieldy, particularly to someone who wasn't used to using it? Or a woman?" Mark asked.

"I would say so."

Mark closed his eyes and leaned back against the wall. "So not the widow, then," he said.

"But she could still be involved," Charley said.

"Of course," Mark said, straightening. "You've been very helpful, Doc. What we need now, Mrs. Hall, is your friend at the newspaper who has the ability to unearth what others try to keep hidden."

"Grace Fletcher, of course! She'll be able to help," Charley said. It wasn't a *Trib* story, but the newspaper's archivist was a wiz at finding and processing information. She'd proven to be an invaluable help to Charley on many stories and, in fact, had been responsible for finding the key piece of information needed to track down Freddie when he'd gone missing. Grace had also introduced her to Laine, her roommate.

"Not this time," Laine said. "At least not until next week. She's gone to visit her family in Cornwall."

"Oh yes, I'd forgotten." It would be two more days before she could talk to Grace. Two more days Dan would have to spend stuck in a cell at the police station. "Drat!"

"I think we've taken up enough of your time, Doc," Mark said. "Thanks for the info. If you hear anything more—"

"I'll be sure to let you know," Laine said, rising. She crossed to the door and released the lock.

Charley hadn't moved. There had to be something more

she could do. She hated feeling helpless. She couldn't help Freddie and now she wasn't sure she could help Dan.

"Mrs. Hall? Charley?"

She rose slowly. Well, maybe there was *something* she could do, if not for Dan, at least for her brother. "Since you're alone this weekend, how'd you like to come for dinner, Laine?"

"Thanks for the offer. I'd love to accept but I'm on call all weekend. That's the reason I didn't go to Cornwall with Grace."

Disappointed, Charley left the lounge, Mark on her heels. She heard him mutter "women" under his breath and whirled around to face him.

"What?" she demanded.

"Please tell me you aren't trying to set up Freddie and the doc."

"And what if I am?"

He shook his head as if pitying her but didn't respond.

It felt like everyone and everything was trying to thwart her efforts to accomplish something—anything. She wasn't sure they were any further ahead in proving Dan's innocence than when they'd arrived on campus. In fact, they seemed to be helping to make the Crown's case. According to Laine, a strong, powerful man, likely familiar with wooden oars, had most likely committed the murder.

Mark seemed neither surprised nor upset by their findings. He'd stated quite blatantly that he wasn't unhappy with Dan's predicament; he was only interested in finding the killer.

But what if they couldn't *prove* that the killer wasn't Dan? Would Mark be okay with that? Because she sure as heck wouldn't be.

He opened the passenger door to his car. "I'm free for dinner, not that you asked," he said mockingly.

Maybe hiring Mark hadn't been a good idea, after all.

"I'm going to walk home," she said, needing to get away from him. Needing time to think.

CHARLEY MOTIONED Irena away as the housekeeper came to greet her. She tossed her straw cartwheel hat on the hall stand. She disliked wearing hats, especially in the summer, but at least this one had a wide enough brim to keep the sun off her face. She lifted her hair off the back of her neck to try to cool down from her walk. There had been a nice breeze along the lakefront, but it had disappeared as she'd turned north for the final part of her journey home.

Charley was relieved to find the drawing room empty. Today's copy of the *Trib* sat unopened on the coffee table. She grabbed it, adding to the *Whig-Standard* she'd purchased on her way home, and sat down in her favourite *bergère* armchair.

MURDER ON THE LOW SEAS:
CANNON CAUGHT IN CATARAQUI CARNAGE

She winced at the overly dramatic headline but wasn't surprised to see it was the main story of the day. She skimmed Lester Pyne's coverage. It contained nothing that hadn't already come out in court. For once, she was happy that Pyne wasn't a dogged journalist able to scent out a scoop. She hoped it meant there wasn't one, but she wasn't so sure. She tossed the paper aside and braced herself as she opened the *Whig-Standard*.

WIDOW WEEPS AS ALDERMAN CANNON
CHARGED IN MURDER OF
FORMER ROWING COACH

Widow?

She sat up straighter and began reading. Sure enough, the competition had managed to get an interview with Georgia Beanish. She could imagine John Sherman's reaction when he found out the *Trib* had been scooped.

According to Georgia Beanish, her husband had gone out in one of his boats early in the morning but promised to be back in time to accompany her to the rowing club's Dominion Day tea. She'd gone to an appointment to get her hair done and returned home around noon. According to the reporter, she was on the verge of hysteria—that was a little much, Charley thought—when she admitted she was annoyed with her husband because he'd obviously lost track of time and wasn't able to take her to the tea.

Charley leaned back. So that meant Beanish returned home and was killed sometime after his wife had left for the rowing club. She glanced at the wedding photograph the paper had run. It showed a young, slightly plump woman with neatly plaited blonde hair, happily gazing up at a much older man. Beanish, for his part, looked absolutely smitten in the photo. She couldn't remember if she'd served Georgia Beanish at the tea, but she had poured for so many people, and there was nothing about the woman that was particularly memorable.

She'd ask around to be sure someone had seen her there. The Crown would likely use her testimony to narrow down the time of death, especially considering what Laine told them about *rigor mortis.*

Dan said he'd left the tea to meet with Beanish after he'd gotten a message from him. If everyone was telling the truth, that left a very small window during which the murder could have taken place.

"Charlotte, thank goodness you're home." Bessie Stormont crossed the room to the sidebar and poured herself a sherry. "Would you like one?"

"Definitely." Charley stood to accept the glass and kissed Gran on the cheek. "Thank you. It's been a trying few days."

"Are you involved in this?" Bessie motioned toward the newspapers that lay open where Charley had dropped them on the floor.

"Not for the *Trib*."

"Well, maybe you should be."

That's surprising.

Gran had made no secret of the fact she didn't think the city beat—especially crime reporting—was something she wanted her granddaughter to do. In fact, she'd been practically giddy with joy when Charley had been demoted to the women's pages.

Bessie bent to pick up the *Whig-Standard,* carried it to the sofa, and sat down. She took a long sip of her sherry and began reading the article. "Hmmm, the *Trib* didn't even mention Georgia in its coverage," she murmured. "Do you think it's because they were being more sensitive to the feelings of the widow?" she asked, glancing up.

Charley snorted with derision. "Hardly. I think Lester Pyne is a lazy so-and-so and got scooped." She took a sip of her own sherry. "You sound like you know her? Georgia Beanish."

"I made a point of meeting her at the tea."

"Because she's new to town?"

"Because she is—was—Frank Beanish's wife."

"You *knew* Frank Beanish?" How was that possible? Gran was fairly progressive in her outlook—at least compared to many of her contemporaries—but Beanish was decades younger and, from what Mark had told her, he was from a totally different social circle.

Bessie sighed heavily. "You were so young when your parents died. I forget how little you know about them."

Charley leaned forward. If there was a gap in her knowledge about her parents, Gran was responsible for it. She'd been so devastated by their deaths, she'd kept very few photographs and rarely spoke about them.

"Frank Beanish was your father's best friend."

Charley choked on her sherry. "Best friend?" she gasped.

"Oh yes, they met at university and were pairs champions for years."

"Best friends *and* rowing partners?" Charley tried to remember if Gran had ever mentioned Beanish before. She was quite sure she hadn't. She had only recently learned her father was a rower, and now, that he had a partner. And that partner was Dan's villainous Frank Beanish. "I guess, I assumed my father rowed singles, like Dan."

"Oh no, they were quite the team. Until the Great War, anyway. When they came back, competing was no longer important to your father, and Frank took up coaching."

Bessie's tone indicated she'd been quite fond of Beanish. Her grandmother was usually a good judge of character, but Dan's interactions with him hadn't been positive at all. Maybe the war had changed him.

"Did they keep in touch when they came back?" Charley asked.

"Oh yes, thick as thieves. Frank got leave to go to England, in 1915, so he could be best man at your parents' wedding. And then your father stood up for him when he married Aggie—Agatha—his first wife, when he returned home. The four of them were very close." She took a sip of her sherry. "He was such a lovely man. Always remembered my birthday and sent me a Christmas card every year, even after your parents died."

"When did you last hear from him?"

"He wrote me a note after he got back to Kingston. He told me he had married again—I was so happy to hear it; I didn't think he'd ever recover from Aggie's death. I was hoping to have a dinner party to introduce them around, but he asked me to wait because Georgia was quite overwhelmed with all the changes from moving to a new country." She withdrew a kerchief from her sleeve and dabbed at her eyes.

"I am having trouble reconciling the man you're describing with the one Dan told me about," Charley said shaking her head. "Did you know Frank Beanish was the coach Dan had fired from the Queen's rowing team after one of the members was horribly hazed? That he blacklisted Dan from the Olympic team last week?"

"I do remember that incident at the university. Rose and I quarrelled over it. We didn't speak to one another for over a year. Frank was going through such a difficult period. I thought the university, indeed the whole rowing community, should have been more lenient."

"A young man almost lost his life! If it hadn't been for Dan—"

"I am not trying to diminish the seriousness of what

happened." Bessie took a deep sip of the sherry. "But Frank was distracted at the time, probably quite incapable of adequately supervising a team of rambunctious young men. That winter he'd lost both Aggie and their daughter to the flu. Their daughter, by the way, was named Cynthia, after your mother."

Bessie paused as if expecting Charley to say something. But Charley had nothing to say. Her heart and her head ached.

"He lost everything: his family, his career. He'd already lost his best friend. With nothing to hold him here, he went to England. I was sorry to see him go—he was my last connection to your father."

"You know Dan has been arrested for his murder."

"Oh, I don't for a second believe Daniel had anything to do with it."

"Well, I am glad to hear that. I was—"

"Excuse me, Mrs. Stormont? Mrs. Hall?" Irena stood in the doorway, her face flushed and her hands fluttering by her side. "There are two RCMP officers here, asking to speak to Mr. Stormont."

"To Freddie?" Charley leapt to her feet. What had her brother gotten himself into this time? "I'll speak with them."

She didn't wait for Gran or Irena to respond. She marched out of the drawing room to the foyer. She didn't recognize the two uniformed men standing at attention in their polished boots with their broad-rimmed hats tucked under their arms. But then most of her contact was with Kingston's local cops, not the federal police.

"I'm Charlotte Stormont Hall. Can I help you?" she asked.

"Good afternoon, ma'am," the taller of the two men said, nodding his head in greeting. "I'm Sergeant Bronson and this is Corporal MacNamara. We really need to speak to Mr. Stormont."

"Is he in trouble?"

"Oh, no, ma'am, nothing like that. We just need to speak to the head of the house—"

"Well, that would be me," Bessie said from behind Charley. "Elizabeth Stormont. This is my house. Whatever this is about, I am sure I am as capable of dealing with it as my grandson."

The two officers glanced at each other, clearly uncomfortable. The tall, talkative one cleared his throat. "I'm sorry Mrs. Stormont, but it's best if we speak with *Mr.* Stormont."

"Oh, for heaven's sake!" Charley turned to Irena. "Is my brother home? Can you go get him, please?"

The housekeeper nodded and hurried past them, up the stairs. Charley figured her brother was probably sleeping off a hangover and would be of little use to the police. But let them find that out for themselves. Gran, in the meantime, was clearly unamused at being sidelined in favour of a junior member of her household. The mere fact she hadn't invited them into the drawing room and offered them tea demonstrated to Charley just how annoyed she was. To her grandmother, leaving someone waiting in a hallway was the worst social snub imaginable.

It took about five uncomfortable minutes for Freddie to appear. He'd obviously been sleeping. His hair was unbrushed and there was a pink indentation from the edge of a sheet stretching across his cheek. He'd managed to dress presentably and was tucking in his shirt as he descended the stairs.

"What's this all about, officers?" he asked jovially.

Charley tried to discern from his posture whether he was concerned about a visit from the Mounties, but it didn't appear so. His shoulders were relaxed and from his expression, she could tell he found it humorous that he'd been elevated above Gran as the recipient of whatever information they had to offer.

"Shall we go into the drawing room?" he said magnanimously and swept his arm forward, indicating they all should precede him.

Gran, head held high and back ramrod straight, led the procession into the drawing room. She was definitely not relaxed, and Charley wondered if Freddie was taking his new-found status too far.

Once they were all seated, he repeated his question.

Sergeant Bronson withdrew a photograph from his pocket and handed it to Freddie. "Do you recognize this boat?"

Freddie shook his head. Charley held out her hand and he passed it to her.

"A sailboat?" She was confused. *Lady Stonebridge* was painted on the stern.

"A sloop," Corporal MacNamara snapped, the first words he'd spoken since the officers arrived.

Bronson gave his subordinate a stern look and turned to Charley. "Mac's our watercraft specialist," he said by way of apology.

"Okay, fine, a *sloop*. But what does it mean?"

Gran had stretched out her hand to take the photo, but as soon as her fingers touched it, she shrieked as if it had burned her, and it fell to the floor.

"I'M NOT sure what seeing the boat is going to accomplish," Charley muttered to Freddie as they followed Sergeant Bronson along the dock. The RCMP officers' visit yesterday had so upset Bessie, she'd immediately retired to her room and hadn't even come down for breakfast this morning.

"It's a sloop," Freddie reminded her. "And you didn't have to come."

Except she did. Finding answers was in her bones and the sudden appearance of this *sloop* after a quarter-century posed so many questions. Bronson knew nothing of its history—only that the name *Lady Stonebridge* was registered to a Frederick Stormont. But the Frederick Stormont the officers had been looking for was dead. And neither Charley nor the Frederick Stormont they'd located had any idea why the abandoned sailboat would be floating in the Cataraqui River.

Her parents had been returning from visiting friends in Cape Vincent, New York, when they were found drowned in Lake Ontario. She assumed the sailboat had capsized, but information was sketchy and reports from the time said it had been a clear, calm evening.

Charley had only been four at the time of the accident and had no real memory of them or of the transition that had happened when she and Freddie had gone to live with Gran and Frederick Senior. Despite Dan's many attempts to get her out on the water, she'd only ever been on one boat in her life—and that was only a few months ago when she'd been searching for Freddie.

She glanced at her brother. While he'd never shown any interest in the family's traditional sport of rowing, or for sailing, he didn't seem to share her fear of the water. Without hesitation, he stepped gracefully into the boat and headed down into the cabin. She remained on the dock with Bronson.

The wooden sloop bobbed calmly in the bay, occasionally knocking against the dock. The mast towered above the craft, its sails lowered and tied securely to the boon. It looked like it could use a fresh coat of paint, the blue of the previous coat having become faded and scratched away in many places. The name along the stern, written in ornate gold lettering, was more prominent, as if it had been recently repainted. *Lady Stonebridge*. What an odd name for a boat.

"So, you don't know where it came from. Or where it's been," she said, unnecessarily summarizing what they'd been told the previous day. Bronson had speculated that it had broken free from its mooring during the sudden violent storm on Dominion Day, but if Freddie hadn't been the one mooring it, they had no idea where it had come from. "What's going to happen to it now?"

"That's up to your brother, I guess. There's no reason for us to keep it."

Freddie's head appeared out of the cabin. "It looks like someone has been taking care of it. Otherwise, I can't imagine it would still be seaworthy."

"Anything to indicate who that would have been?" Charley called to him.

Freddie leapt back onto the dock. "No, nothing."

"What are we going to do with it?"

"I think I might take up sailing."

"Oh, Freddie, no!"

Ignoring her protest, he turned to the sergeant. "How long can you keep her here? I need to find a berth for her."

"Maybe a week."

"There must be some record of what happened to it after the accident," Charley insisted. "There has to be a record of the investigation that was done. Two people died." Not for the first time, she was frustrated by the lack of information her grandparents had provided about her parents' deaths. She'd read everything the *Trib* had published about the accident when she'd started as a copy editor at the newspaper, but it wasn't much more than tributes to her parents' good works.

Bronson shrugged. "Sorry, Mrs. Hall. I had Corporal MacNamara go through our files after we met with you yesterday, and we simply don't have any information about your parents' accident."

After an entirely unsatisfactory morning, Charley decided to turn her focus toward something more proactive. She'd called the police station and was relieved to discover the sergeant on duty was Jerry Kearn, a kind-hearted soul whom she thought wasn't truly cut out for police work. Kearn agreed to let her visit Dan "briefly." She suspected he felt sorry for the alderman who was stuck in the station's holding cells until his trial, which was scheduled to begin later in the week. Still, she was grateful and stopped at one of the bakery stalls in the market to purchase some fresh cinnamon cakes to show her appreciation.

"Something smells good," Dan said, shuffling into the Sergeant's Office. He looked better than she'd expected. He was clean-shaven and was dressed in one of his own neatly pressed suits. If it wasn't for the shackles, she'd think he was ready for a normal day at the office—except, also, for the lack of a belt and tie.

Charley started toward him, then paused and looked at Sergeant Kearn who had stationed himself behind the desk in the corner of the room. He glanced up from the cake he'd picked up and shrugged his shoulders, which she took as a sign he wouldn't stop her from giving Dan a hug.

She wrapped her arms around her friend and lay her head against his chest. With the shackles, his arms couldn't encircle her, so he rested them on her hips.

"I'm fine. I'm fine." He spoke softly and repeated the phrase several times as if he thought that would somehow alleviate her concerns.

The sergeant cleared his throat and she released him.

"Do you have to stay here?" she asked Kearn.

"I'm afraid so. But I'll just be reading some papers and enjoying this lovely cake. You won't even know I'm here."

"Come over here and sit down," Dan said, taking her hand and leading her to one of two chairs across the room.

She managed to snag one of the small cakes and handed it to Dan. "Is it awful?" she asked.

"No, not at all. The fellas here are very hospitable, isn't that right Jerry?" Dan gave her his politician's smile. "He's quite the card shark, you know. You're going to make a fortune off me, aren't you Jer?"

"I'm not listening," Jerry replied, keeping his head down, but his lips were twitching.

"Stop it, Dan." She wasn't buying his happy-go-lucky act. "This isn't a luxury vacation. You're in serious trouble."

Dan sobered. "Dwelling on the bad stuff isn't going to help me. I need to stay positive. I didn't kill Beanish. I will be proven innocent."

"Are the police even looking for another suspect?" She glanced at Jerry, but he now seemed to be earnestly engrossed in a report he was reading.

Dan shook his head. "I don't think so. That's why I'm counting on you to find something that will get their attention. Given Beanish's character, it shouldn't be too hard to find someone else who had a beef with him."

Beanish's character.

After what Gran had told her about Beanish's relationship with her father, Charley was having great difficulty seeing the murdered man as the villain Dan claimed he was. How could one man garner completely opposite reactions in the two people whose opinions she trusted most?

Dan hated Beanish, but he was right: someone else must have hated him more.

"How's it going, anyway?" Dan asked.

"I am trying to pin down the time of death. I think that's key." Charley leaned back. "His widow says he took the boat out earlier in the day and he hadn't returned when she left for the tea, around 1 p.m. So, he had to have been killed after that. You arrived when?"

"Probably close to four."

"Okay, so that's a three-hour window. You rowed across the river, right? Was his boat there when you arrived?"

"Jeepers, Charley. How many times do I have to tell you, we don't row *boats*? They're sculls. And yes, his *scull* was there when I arrived."

"Fine." Charley bristled at the rebuke. What was it about men and their boats? Both MacNamara and Freddie had corrected her, too: It was a *sloop*, not a sailboat. As far as she was concerned, if it floated on water it was a boat.

"I can confirm that there were two single-person sculls on the scene when we arrived," Kearn said from across the room. "One belonging to the victim and the other to Mr. Cannon."

"Thank you." Charley gave him an appreciative smile. "Can you tell me who called you to go to the scene and when?"

"Sorry, ma'am, I shouldn't have said anything. Pretend I'm not here." Kearn gave her an apologetic half-smile and returned his gaze to whatever he was reading.

"Okay, then." She turned back to Dan. "What time did Beanish call *you* to go visit him?"

"I don't know. I didn't actually speak to him. He left a message with Diana and she told me when she arrived for the tea."

"So, it's possible Beanish never made the call at all," Charley mused.

"What are you saying? You think someone else lured me there?"

"I'm thinking out loud." Charley stood and began pacing the room. She did her best analyzing when she was in motion. "Why wouldn't Beanish call you directly? And why ask you to come to him? Why not talk to you at the rowing club tea, since he was supposed to be there?"

"If it wasn't Beanish, I would know from the voice on the phone," Dan said, spinning in his chair to face her.

"Exactly!"

"Okay, let's say someone else did make the call. Why?"

"To throw suspicion for the murder on someone else, I would presume."

"But why me?"

Charley stopped and leaned against the wall. Two thoughts occurred to her. "Your history with Beanish is well known. Perhaps you were simply an easy mark."

"I suppose that's possible."

Charley hesitated to raise the other, more sinister possibility. But she needed Dan's help. "Or someone has a vendetta against both you and Beanish. Killing him and having you take the fall would give him his retribution."

In many ways, she hoped the first scenario would prove true. She didn't want to think someone could hate Dan so much as to have him hang for a crime he hadn't committed. However, without a clear motive for specifically framing him, the killer could be anybody, making it nearly impossible to save Dan.

She returned to her chair and leaned toward him. "Can you think of anyone who would have it in for the two of you?"

Dan looked visibly shaken. "Beanish has been gone—out of the country—for almost ten years. I only saw him once after his return—last weekend at the regatta in St. Catharines."

"Think further back."

The shackles jangled noisily as Dan raised a hand to his face and rubbed his eyes wearily. The devil-may-care attitude was gone.

"I did hear that Donnelly—what was the kid's first name? Jack? Jake? Sorry, it's slipped my mind. He was involved in that hazing incident all those years ago. I heard he'd fallen on hard times."

"Was he one of the rowers who got kicked off the team?"

"None of the rowers got kicked off the team. Only the coach. Donnelly was the kid who was hazed."

Finally, Monday!

Charley might actually get something accomplished. Grace would be back, and the city would be returning to business-as-usual.

Charley hurried through her morning routine. She'd have a quick cup of coffee with Gran—a familial requirement that somehow Freddie always managed to avoid—and then head to the *Trib*. She had to do a write-up about the Dominion Day tea, *ugh*, but it was necessary if she had any hope of getting Sherman to publish her more important article calling for improved social supports for seniors, especially women, who more often than not found themselves isolated and destitute after their husbands died.

And she had an arm's-length list of questions about both Beanish's murder and the mysterious *Lady Stonebridge* she needed answered.

She sped down the stairs and stopped short on the threshold to the dining room. The dark-haired man turned his head at her gasp, and then rose from his seat and approached her.

"Good morning, Mrs. Hall," Mark said, pulling out a chair for her.

"Detective, I don't remember asking you to meet me

here." She glanced anxiously at her grandmother. Bessie knew she'd been helping Dan, but she didn't want her grandmother to know how involved Charley was in trying to prove his innocence, and she wanted to keep it that way.

"You didn't." Mark returned to his seat and took a healthy scoop of eggs from the platter. "I will miss Chantal's chocolate cake, but your new housekeeper does a wonderful job with scrambled eggs," he said, raising his fork as if toasting her.

"Good morning, Charlotte. I hope you slept well." Bessie's tone held a reprimand. She demanded a certain level of etiquette, which included banal pleasantries before business.

"Yes, good morning, Gran. I'm sorry. I slept well, thank you. And you?"

"Very well, thank you."

Charley watched impatiently as Gran slowly lifted her coffee cup to her lips and took a sip. She needed to wait until Gran raised the issue of Mark's presence.

Irena arrived with a fresh pot of coffee and poured Charley a cup. Mark waved her away; apparently, or maybe incredulously, he'd had his fill.

Just how long has he been here?

"I asked the detective to join us for breakfast," Gran said, finally.

"Oh. Do you want him to look into why my parents' sailboat—*sloop*—suddenly reappeared?" Charley had assumed her grandmother had felt the matter was closed since she hadn't said a word about the boat since the RCMP officers' visit. She was pleased to know Gran was taking more of an interest in its mysterious discovery.

"No, I've hired him to find Frank Beanish's killer."

The words hit Charley like a brick, and she swung her

head back to glare at Mark. Why hadn't he told Gran he was already working on the case? Did he expect to collect two fees for doing the same work?

"Sailboat?" he asked.

"It's nothing." Gran pushed her chair back and Mark leapt to his feet to help her up. "I need to send a note and some flowers to Mrs. Beanish, and then I have a mountain of correspondence to catch up on." She paused to kiss Charley on the cheek. "Have a good day, dear."

Charley waited until she was certain Gran was out of earshot. "What are you playing at?"

Mark shrugged. "I'm not playing at anything. Your grandmother offered me a job and I accepted it."

"But *I* hired you to help me solve the murder."

"No. You hired me to help you prove the alderman didn't do it. Your grandmother hired me to find the killer."

"But it's the same thing!"

"Maybe." Mark's eyes darkened and a furrow formed between his heavy black eyebrows. "Maybe not."

Charley bit back her annoyance. He could nuance it any way he wanted, but she was sure they were working toward the same end. Freeing Dan was the only thing that mattered and if that meant putting up with Mark's not-so-veiled animosity for his half-brother, so be it.

"So, what's our next move?" she asked.

"There is no 'our'," he said, rising to leave. "I work alone."

"Oh no you don't!" Charley pushed back her chair and positioned herself at the entryway of the dining room to block his exit. "I have information from Dan that you don't. You need me."

He stopped mere inches from her. He was intimidating.

She knew that's how he wanted her to feel. And he'd succeeded, to a point: intimidated *yes*, threatened *no*.

"Mrs. Hall," he said in a low, aggrieved tone, "I am a trained detective. I've spent over ten years with the Toronto Police Department. I've worked on, and solved, more homicides than you can possibly imagine. I sincerely doubt that an accused murderer, looking to escape the hangman's noose, could provide you with any information on the crime that I couldn't obtain on my own."

How dare he!

Dan may be accused, but he was *not* a murderer. And as for the hangman's noose? Well, that wasn't an option. And darn it, she did have information Mark didn't have. But going on the offensive wasn't going to help her. She could find Beanish's real killer without Mark, but it would be so much easier with his expertise, even if he didn't fully believe Dan was innocent.

Kindness not knives.

"But we make a good team," she said, trying to keep her tone conciliatory. "I was the one who figured out who killed Marjorie Dixon. You found Freddie. But it was teamwork—you and me working together—that led to both of those solutions."

From his scowl, she could tell he wasn't buying it.

"You took me to see Laine Black!" Desperation crept into her voice.

"When I took you to see the doc, you were my client." He reached into his pocket and handed her an envelope—her envelope, containing the fee she had paid him to help her. "As I am no longer working for you, I am not obligated to have you tag along." He gently nudged her out of his way and stepped past her. "Besides, your grandmother made it very clear: She does not want you involved in this."

CHARLEY WAS STILL FUMING when she arrived at the *Trib*'s offices on Bath Street. She shook out her umbrella. The rainy day matched her mood.

Who does he think he is to dismiss me like a nobody?

How can Gran do this to me?

She'd show them. She was as good an investigator as Mark ever was! And she had Grace.

She glanced around the newsroom, her gaze automatically landing on her former desk where Lester Pyne, enveloped by his usual halo of cigarette smoke, was typing away.

Does he have something?

She started towards him but John Sherman's "Hall!" stopped her. She turned toward her editor and obeyed his non-verbal, cocked-head command to step into his office.

She closed the door and turned to face him. "What's up, boss?"

"Your story on the alderman's disappearance was a little light."

She fidgeted uncomfortably, fearing where this was heading. Sherman wasn't wrong. She'd downplayed the story, providing only the facts without mentioning the reason for Dan's last-minute decision to go to the Philadelphia regatta. But it hadn't been much of a story. Until Beanish had wound up dead and Dan was charged with his murder.

Sherman pushed his wire-rimmed glasses up onto his head and rubbed his eyes. "Look, Hall, I know he's a personal friend—"

"Which you've used to your advantage in the past," Charley said to remind Sherman that she'd allowed him to exploit their friendship for the *Trib*.

"But this is a big deal. Murder is a big deal."

"He didn't do it!"

"The evidence seems to suggest otherwise. I know you've been to see him. Do you have anything you can give us? I don't want to be scooped by the *Whig* again. I don't know how they got to the widow so fast." He shook his head and heaved a deep sigh. "He must have told you things. Even if we could have his side of the story—"

"You want me to write about my personal conversation with him?"

"No, of course not," Sherman said quickly. "But there must be something the alderman told you. Something you could pass on to Pyne."

"No!" Charley glared at him. "I know you want a scoop, but I don't have one. Dan is innocent. Have Pyne write that."

Sherman rounded the desk and raised his hands in a placating gesture as if he thought that would calm the situation. "This is a huge story in the city," he cajoled. "It's going to get written one way or the other. You can influence the tone. Help choose what aspects get coverage."

Charley didn't even try to hide her contempt as she gazed down at her boss. She had a good two inches on him —even without her modest-heeled pumps. She resented

Sherman's decision to replace her with Pyne, but she'd been a good egg and had fed him more than one scoop over the past few months. But this was going too far. "You're right, this is a big story. And I'm sorry Lester Pyne isn't up to snuff. But the city is no longer my beat and I have my own stories to work on." And in case he hadn't gotten the point, she slammed Sherman's office door on her way out.

"Oh, hey, Mrs. Hall," Pyne called to her as she crossed the newsroom. "Can I have a word?"

"Sorry. Busy," she yelled back, refusing to slow down or even look at him as she made her way to the back corner of the *Trib's* offices where its archives—dubbed the morgue—was situated.

"I hate men!" Charley said, entering the long, dark room without bothering to knock.

Archivist Grace Fletcher looked up from the stack of newspapers she'd been sorting through and grinned. "All men or one in particular?"

"At the moment three," Charley said, counting off Mark, Sherman and Pyne in her head. And she wasn't too happy with Freddie and his decision to take up sailing, either. "And a half."

"Come have a seat and I'll pour you a cup of tea," Grace said. "Tell me what's going on with you."

Charley repeated her conversation with Sherman while she watched Grace prepare the tea. Grace was younger than Charley but seemed to have mastered the ability to project a serene self-assurance that was generally found in someone much older.

"He may have a point, you know," Grace said, placing a teapot on the worktable. "But I wouldn't give it to Pyne. He's a hack. He will only butcher it."

"I am not going to take advantage of our friendship just to give the *Trib* a scoop."

"That's not what I'm saying." Grace poured a drop of tea into her cup, nodded with approval, and poured and handed a cup to Charley. "Your words have the power to influence people. No, hear me out," she said when Charley started to protest. "Fiona MacDonald would have hanged if it hadn't been for your article about her difficult childhood and the tough life she's had since she came to Canada. You made people see her as a real person and understand why and how she was driven to do what she did."

"She was still found guilty of murder."

"Of course, because she *was* guilty." Grace chuckled. "But thirty years in prison is far more preferable than a death sentence. She'll be in her fifties when she's released. She's content with that. And who knows what kind of world we'll have by then? Maybe she will be able to pursue her medical degree, after all."

Even though the woman had tried to kill her, Charley's heart ached for Fiona. She'd been driven to murder believing it was the only way she could protect her family and others from the dangerously misguided philosophy of a woman who thought she was saving troubled souls. Charley regularly visited Fiona and, thanks to Laine, often brought her medical textbooks to help pass the time.

"And, don't forget your articles also resulted in Fiona's younger brother and sister being adopted by a nice family in Harrowsmith, rather than having to go live in an orphanage."

"Okay, I concede your point. But Dan is innocent. I just need to find some evidence to prove it *before* they convict him."

"Which is why you're here."

"Am I that transparent?" Charley grinned. "Maybe I simply wanted to welcome you back."

"Welcome accepted, but Laine gave me a heads-up. I've been doing a bit of digging into Frank Beanish. He was quite wealthy, you know."

"But he was working as a fireman for the railroad in England."

"Who knows what motivates people. If he was working, it was because he wanted to, not because he needed to." A furrow formed between Grace's brows and she hesitated. "He was a friend of your father's. Did you know that?"

"I only just found out from Gran."

"His family made their money in plastics. He sold the family business in '39 and left the country a few months before England declared war on the Nazis."

"Do you know anything about his new wife?"

Grace shrugged. "It takes time to get messages overseas, I'm afraid."

"Anything about a will? Life insurance policy?"

Grace shook her head. "I can do some digging, but don't hold your breath. That kind of information is difficult to get."

"Well, at least I know where Frank Beanish's money came from. And presumably the new Mrs. Beanish knew her husband was well off when she married him, which could go to motive."

"I'll keep digging into Beanish's life. Maybe I can find someone else who had a beef with him."

"Dan did give me the name of a rower from his Queen's University days. A Jake or Jack Donnelly. I looked in the city directory and there is a J. Donnelly listed on Bagot Street, so I'll check him out."

Charley didn't know where it would lead. Donnelly

may hold a grudge against his teammates for the hazing and the coach who'd allowed it to happen, but what would he have against Dan, who had not only rescued him but insisted Beanish be held accountable? Had something happened more recently that would make Dan suspicious of him? He'd have told her, wouldn't he?

"You look very serious," Grace said.

"It's nothing," Charley said. She had no reason to doubt Dan. She was sure she'd understand once she spoke with Donnelly. "There is something else I'd like you to check into for me, though."

"About Alderman Cannon's case?"

"No, something totally unrelated." Charley paused to take a sip of her tea. It was time, she decided. After these many years, it looked as though the questions around her parents' deaths were ready to be answered. "The boat my parents were sailing when they died suddenly appeared in the Cataraqui River over the weekend."

"That's odd."

"Yeah. The Mounties don't know where it came from and they're not particularly interested in pursuing the mystery. I'm wondering if it's possible to find out where the sloop ended up all those years ago and why it suddenly turned up here."

"There was an investigation into your parents' deaths, right?"

"Their bodies were discovered on the American side of the lake, so it was a New York State investigation. The RCMP has no record of it."

"I'm not sure I'll be able to do much about it today. Yesterday was Independence Day and the Yanks are probably still celebrating or sleeping it off. But leave it with me. I love a challenge."

Romeo Arcadi's taxi was idling in the driveway when Charley returned home mid-afternoon. It had been a productive day, despite failing to connect with J. Donnelly. She'd called his telephone number several times but there'd been no answer.

She'd taken her portable red typewriter and set up in a corner of the morgue. She missed the hubbub of the newsroom, but it was the only thing she could think to do to avoid both Sherman and Pyne. She couldn't—or wouldn't—give them what they wanted, and she wasn't up to arguing about it. She didn't know how she'd handle tomorrow, but she'd face that hurdle when it arrived.

Arcadi rolled down his window as she approached. She angled her umbrella to keep the rain off both of them as he crossed his arms on the ledge and leaned out to greet her.

"Your grandmother called," he said. "Oh, here she comes now. Excuse me."

Charley backed up to allow him out of the cab. He opened a very large, black umbrella and escorted Gran, and a very large casserole dish, off the front porch and to the cab.

"Where are you going?" Charley asked, coming up on her other side.

Bessie looked annoyed. "I am going to call on Mrs. Beanish if you must know." Arcadi opened the door and took the casserole dish as Bessie settled herself onto the back seat.

Charley raced around to the other side, opened the door and, deftly closing her umbrella, slid in beside her grandmother.

"What do you think you're doing?" Gran demanded.

"I'm coming with you. To pay my respects."

Arcadi took his place in the driver's seat and turned towards Bessie, an eyebrow cocked inquisitively. Gran waved him on, and he put the taxi into reverse and backed down the driveway.

Gran turned to Charley. "Let me be perfectly clear, Charlotte. This is a social call. The woman has just lost her husband and is grieving. If you have any thoughts about questioning her about the murder or anything, *and I mean anything,* that could be related to it, you are not to get out of this cab. Leave the investigation work to Detective Spadina. I simply want to offer her some comfort. Do you understand?"

Charley nodded. Her first thought had been to interrogate the widow, but Gran was right. Now wasn't the time. Still, she could learn about her life in England, how she and Beanish met and fell in love, why they had come back to Canada. All legitimate topics. Gran could hardly chastise her for showing interest in the newcomer. Once they had a rapport, she could come back on her own and press for the answers she needed.

The Georgia Beanish who answered the door didn't much resemble the woman from the photo in the newspaper. Her blonde hair looked as if she'd made a quick attempt to tie it back, but many of her corkscrew curls had escaped their binding. Her eyes were pink and puffy and her nose, already on the large size, was made even more prominent by the reddish hue it had taken on from being rubbed raw with too many tissues. She wore a simple, brown housedress and flats. Charley knew she was about her own age, but she seemed so much older. Maybe it was her accent; not all English accents could be called sophisticated, but hers definitely reminded Charley of the speeches given over the radio by King George.

"Thank you for this," Georgia said, accepting the casserole dish after the introductions were made. "I sent the girl home. I'm not used to being fussed over."

"That's quite all right, my dear," Gran said. "We won't stay. We only wanted to see how you were doing and if there was anything you need."

"Where are my manners? Please come in. Frank was so fond of you, Mrs. Stormont. It would be nice to talk to people who knew him so well. I can make us some tea. And some of the women from the rowing club dropped off biscuits—cookies, you call them, I think." She turned and led them through the house into the kitchen.

Charley watched in fascination as Georgia set about to prepare tea. Bessie seemed equally intrigued that the woman knew where everything was stored—tea, kettle, cups, dishes. She even knew how to light the stove, something Charley was certain her grandmother had never done herself.

Georgia must have noticed their bemused expression as she set a plate of chocolate chip cookies down on the table. "Frank always found it funny, too, that I insisted on preparing our meals. I'm not used to living with the comfort of a cook." She gave a small smile as she joined them at the table. "Although I have found it much easier to get used to having someone else doing the laundry. I don't miss that one bit."

"How did you and Mr. Beanish meet?" Charley asked, ignoring Gran's pointed glare.

Georgia self-consciously patted her hair as a faint blush crept up her cheeks. "You must be wondering what a gentleman like him would see in me?"

"Actually, I was wondering the opposite," Charley said. "What did you see in a man almost twice your age?"

"Charlotte!" Gran's voice cracked like a whip.

Had she gone too far?

"Oh, it's all right, Mrs. Stormont. I am not offended. It's a fair question. May I call you Charlotte? You didn't know him, did you? He said he'd never met you—well, that's not true. He said he hadn't seen you since you were a toddler."

"I don't remember him at all."

"It's true, he was older than I am. And he didn't have movie-star good looks. But he had—what do the Americans call it?—charisma? Yes! He had charisma. In spades."

Charley waited while she paused to pour out the tea.

"Milk? Sugar? I must admit, I am having difficulty getting used to such luxuries. We still have food rationing back home." She added a generous amount of both to her tea and stirred thoughtfully before picking up her story. "According to my mum, Frank caught the eye of many a widow when he first arrived in Feltham."

"You weren't living there at the time?"

"No, I was still in London." A shadow passed across her face. "I moved back home Christmas 1940. My husband and son had both been killed in the blitz that autumn."

"Oh, my dear, I am so sorry." Gran reached across the table and took Georgia's hands. "You have suffered such tragedy."

"As have you," Georgia said. "Frank told me about your son and daughter-in-law. And that for a time you thought your grandson had died in the war, too." She glanced toward Charley. "We had that in common, Frank and me. We had both lost not only the love of our life but also a child —each would be a devastating blow, but losing both at the same time is almost unbearable."

And now another loss...

The return home was a quiet one as Charley tried to sort through her impressions of Georgia Beanish. Against her better judgment, she found herself liking the young woman. She seemed genuinely fond of her husband but had all but admitted they had come together as a way to lessen their grief rather than actually falling in love with one another. That wasn't necessarily a bad thing. Charley hadn't been in love with Theo when she'd married him. People got married for all sorts of reasons. Just because it wasn't love didn't necessarily make Georgia a killer.

Irena hurried to greet them in the foyer. She helped Bessie remove her coat and took her hat. She turned to Charley and held out her arms to receive Charley's damp coat and hat, as well.

"An envelope came for you, Mrs. Hall," she said. "It's on the hall stand."

Charley nodded her thanks and watched Irena disappear back through the house.

"Charlotte, will you join me for a sherry in the drawing room?" Gran interrupted her thoughts.

"Yes, you go ahead. I'll only be a moment."

The envelope bore the *Kingston Tribune*'s masthead.

Thank you, Grace!

She tore it open and withdrew two typewritten pages of numbers and a newspaper article. She scanned them several times, wondering why on earth Grace would send her financial statements from the Frontenac Rowing Club. Then she saw it. One needn't be an accountant to see that the club was in serious financial trouble. She turned to the newspaper article, published a month ago under Sports Editor Stan Martin's byline:

CARTER RESIGNATION STUNS
ROWING COMMUNITY

"Mr. Carter will see you now."

Charley crossed the waiting room and entered the bank manager's office. Robin Carter rose from behind an enormous wooden desk which dwarfed the surprisingly small room. She'd have thought a bank manager would merit a larger space, but then again, this was a small branch located outside of Kingston's main business core. Still, given the man's height and his generous desk, the office felt claustrophobic.

"Mrs. Hall. Please have a seat and tell me how I can help you today."

Charley took a seat and looked closer at the man she'd only ever seen once before, and that had been across a crowded room when he'd made his laborious farewell speech. He was smartly dressed in a teal-colored, double-breasted suit that emphasized his broad shoulders and trim waist, a bright white shirt and teal-patterned tie. A thin, dark mustache lined his top lip and a thinning ring of grey hair circled around from the back of his head to the top of his ears. Bright blue eyes peered out from heavy-rimmed black glasses.

She'd been surprised by how easily she'd gotten in to see

him. But his assistant hadn't asked the reason for her visit and she hadn't volunteered it.

"I want to talk to you about the rowing club," Charley said.

"Oh, wonderful. I was hoping that's why you were here." Carter sat down. "Is the *Trib* planning to do a profile about me and my tenure there? Twenty-five years as president. A feat that is unmatched and likely never will be."

"I am only beginning my research." Charley smoothly slid into her reporter persona. "I am wondering why you would step down, now, at such a challenging time in the club's history."

Carter cocked his head to the side and pursed his lips.

Charley didn't say anything. He was probably waiting for her to give him more information, but she had no intention of doing so. She knew most people were uncomfortable with silence and often rushed to fill the void with information they hadn't intended to share.

"I am not sure what you mean by challenging times," Carter said eventually.

"Well, the club is facing some financial difficulties, and then, of course, there is the murder of Frank Beanish and the arrest of another member. That type of publicity can be harmful."

Carter stood suddenly. "I don't know where you are getting your information, Mrs. Hall, but you are incorrect. The club is fine. And as for the death of Mr. Beanish, that has absolutely nothing to do with us. It was a private dispute between two members."

Charley reached into her pocketbook and withdrew the financial statements Grace had provided her, holding them up for Carter to see. "According to these papers, the club is close to bankruptcy."

"Where did you get those?"

Charley slowly got to her feet. "I don't know how a respected member of the banking community could have allowed the club's finances to get so out of hand."

He rounded his desk and wrenched open the office door. "Get out!"

"Did Beanish find out about it? Did he blow the whistle on you? Is that why you resigned." Charley kept firing questions at him as he took her arm and ushered her out the door, slamming it behind her.

"Well, that seemed to go well," Mark said dryly, rising from a chair outside the office.

"What are you doing here?"

"Apparently, I've heard the same rumours as you." He glanced at the closed door. "But I don't suppose there's any point in me trying to get answers from him now that you've shown our hand."

Our hand?

"Who's been feeding you rumours?" Charley asked. She was pretty certain she knew, and that only added to her disappointment.

Mark took her arm and escorted her out. "Your grandmother simply said it was strange that Robin Carter would resign now, without much warning," he said in a low voice.

"He's been president for twenty-five years," she whispered back.

He held open the bank's front door and followed her out onto the sidewalk.

"According to Bessie—and yes, we are on a first-name basis—he had barely started his sixth consecutive five-year term and there is no clear successor. She heard rumours that the club was in some financial difficulty and wondered if that was why Carter was leaving."

"Has she figured out how it connects to Beanish's murder?" Charley asked sarcastically. Gran liked to pretend she was oblivious to what she referred to as the "ugliness" of the city's crime beat, but she seemed pretty well-informed about this case. It frustrated Charley that her own grandmother hadn't bothered to share her suspicions with her.

Mark chuckled. "She does wonder if his return has something to do with the discovery of the irregularities."

"And maybe his death."

Mark shrugged. "It could go to motive. Except Carter was speaking at the time of the murder and there are a hundred people—including you—who can provide an alibi for him."

"It doesn't mean he wasn't involved in some way. Or that the finances of the club aren't the real motive for the killing."

"How involved was your alderman in the running of the rowing club? Did he know what was going on?"

"I know where you're going with this, and you're wrong." She scowled at him.

Mark held up his hands. "You're very loyal to your friends, Tiger, and it's an admirable quality in a human being. But it can be a detriment to an investigator. It can blind you to their faults, too. And everyone has faults."

"Even you, Detective?"

Mark chuckled. "I may have one or two."

"Do tell." Charley was intrigued. Mark rarely spoke about himself.

"That's a conversation for another day. Right now, I am going to do you a favour." He took her arm and propelled her along the sidewalk to his car.

"You aren't taking me home, are you? Because regardless of what Gran told you, I am not going to stop trying to clear Dan's name."

Mark opened the passenger door. "I never doubted it." He closed the door after she got in and climbed into the driver's seat beside her. "Carter was never going to give us anything."

"Then why were you here to see him?"

"I wanted to rattle his cage a little. Put him on notice. Make him jumpy. Maybe he'll do something stupid." He revved the engine and pulled out into traffic. "However, since you so kindly did that for me, I am going to allow you to tag along while I interview someone who will likely give us some answers."

CHARLEY FOLLOWED THE SHORT, wiry septuagenarian into the rowing club. Mark had barely had time to introduce him as John Boomer Watson, the club's secretary, before he ushered them into the building and set off toward his office in the back.

She paused in front of a glass display cabinet showing highlights from the club's long history. Gran had said there were photos of her father prominently on display. It was easy to recognize the young man she'd only ever seen in photographs. He was standing beside another man, both with huge grins on their faces as they hoisted a large, cup-shaped trophy above their heads. In a second photograph, he was standing with the same man, their arms raised and victory medals around their necks.

"Ah, that was the summer of 1914," Watson said from behind her.

"Who is the man he's standing beside? Is that Frank Beanish?"

"It sure is. Your father and Beanish made one of the strongest teams we'd ever seen. 'Fred and Frank, Frontenac's Fabulous Phenoms' we called them. We were all certain they were destined for a medal at the '16 Olympics. Of course, that didn't happen."

"Kind of hard to hold an Olympics in a country the world is at war with." Mark had joined them. "They were set for Berlin."

"So, they would have been a double scull?" Charley asked, trying to use the terminology Dan always insisted on.

"No. They didn't scull. They were what we call a straight pair." Watson chuckled. "But good try."

"What's the difference?"

"Rigging. In sculling, a rower has two oars—what we call sculls—one for each side of the boat. In a sweep boat, each rower has only one." He pointed at a photograph of two men in a long, narrow boat, each holding a single oar. "Your father sat bow and rowed starboard. Beanish was strokeside. Straight pairs is a challenging event because each rower's strokes must be evenly matched or they'll go round and round in circles, and there's no coxswain to steer or give commands—but then, I may be biased."

"Coxswain? Is that what you did?" Charley asked.

"That's why they call me Boomer. I wasn't much of a rower," Watson held out his hands presenting his somewhat diminutive size, "but they never missed a cue when I was calling. I crewed with your grandpa, you know."

"No, I didn't. What did he row?"

"He did both fours and eights. There are no photos from way back then on display, but I wrote a history of the club a few years back and there are some in the book. He was one of the founders of the club, you know. I'll see if I can find a copy for you."

Sculls. Sloops. Sweeps. Boys and their boats!

She might have an easier time keeping the names straight in her head if they didn't all begin with the letter S. But maybe she shouldn't criticize. Fred and Frank, Frontenac's Fabulous Phenoms sounded good, but the grammarian in her cringed at the P in the alliteration.

"Sorry for the mess," Watson said when they arrived at his office. He lifted a box of files off one of the chairs and motioned for Charley to take a seat. "I can get another chair."

"I'll stand," Mark said, remaining close to the door.

"As you wish." Watson glanced around the room. "Now where...? Oh yes, here they are." He bent down and retrieved a brown-covered book from a box in the corner, holding it up triumphantly as he moved to his desk. "Shall I inscribe it for you?" Not waiting for an answer, he picked up a pen and with a flourish of his hand began writing on an inside page. When he was done, he held it out to Charley, open to the page he'd signed.

We remember the past, we celebrate the future.
May the Stormont tradition continue along with the club.
Sincerely, Boomer Watson

Not if I have anything to do with it. Charley kept her thoughts to herself and thanked Watson. She closed the book and noted the title, *A History of the Frontenac Rowing Club, 1881–1941 by John Boomer Watson.*

"The first sixty years," Watson mused. "I wrote it for something to do after I retired. The missus told me I was interfering with her running of the house and I needed to find a place to go and something to do every day." A shadow crossed his face. "I don't imagine I'll be around to write the seventy-fifth." Then he seemed to shake off his melancholy, reached into his shirt pocket and withdrew a pocket watch, holding it up proudly. "Over forty years at the shipyard, and

I never missed a day. They gave me this as a thank you when I retired."

"It's lovely," Charley said.

He nodded and put it back in his pocket. "It was a great place to work. We were treated like family. That's why I don't believe for one second that Dan Cannon killed Frank Beanish." He glanced at Mark. "I am assuming that's why you're here, Detective? To ask me about the murder?"

Charley's eyes narrowed as she looked back at Mark. Did Watson think Mark was still a police officer? Shouldn't he identify himself as a *private* detective?

"You knew both men. What can you tell us about them?" Mark said, ignoring Charley's frown.

"Good men. Both of them. They may have had their disagreements, but Dan Cannon isn't a killer. He doesn't have it in him."

"We don't always know a person's true character," Mark countered. "Anyone is capable of murder given the right circumstances."

Watson's eyes widened in surprise and he sat back. "I guess you've seen your fair share of human depravity, Detective."

"More than I care to remember. Now, tell me a bit about each man. Did you ever see them together?"

"No. Because of his work for both his father and the city, Cannon would row very early in the mornings. Beanish coached at the club, so he went out during the day and sometimes in the evenings."

"I remember Dan practicing early when Beanish was his coach," Charley said. "Are you sure they wouldn't have crossed paths?"

Watson scratched his head. "Well, I suppose it's possible. I haven't been an early bird in years. But even if that were the case, Beanish would be busy with whoever he was coaching, and Cannon was off by himself."

"Why don't you tell me about the club's financial problems," Mark said, shifting the conversation.

"Oh—oh dear." Watson looked anxiously between the two of them. "How do you know about that? We've been trying to keep things hush-hush. So embarrassing." His eyes met Charley's. "You aren't planning on writing about it, are you? In your newspaper?"

"No, not at all," Charley reassured him.

"Oh good." He sighed with relief. "Then why are you asking about it?"

"Is it a coincidence that one club member is accused of killing another club member just as the club is facing financial ruin?" Mark asked.

"Financial ruin is a bit overstated, Detective," Watson said defensively. "But there is absolutely no connection between Cannon or Beanish and our finances. In fact, I don't even think they knew about it. Only a very few people in the club do."

"Who?"

"Well, me as secretary along with the president and vice-president."

"Treasurer?" Mark asked.

"Ah, yes, well that's the crux of the matter, isn't it? In hindsight, it was probably a mistake to allow the president to be treasurer."

"Wait a minute." Charley sat forward. "Are you telling me Robin Carter was both president and treasurer? Isn't that a bit unusual?"

"You have to understand, Mrs. Hall, we are a very small

club and not a lot of people step forward to volunteer." Watson squared his shoulders and sat up straighter in his chair, the confident posture belied by the pink hue flushing his face.

"To be clear: are you confirming that the financial irregularities are the result of embezzlement?" Mark asked.

Watson took out a handkerchief and mopped his forehead.

"Was Robin Carter responsible?" Mark went on.

Watson frowned but nodded in affirmation.

"How did you find out about it?" Mark asked. "Was it Beanish that brought it to your attention? He hadn't been back for very long. Is that why it was only recently discovered?"

"Oh, heavens to Betsy, no!" Watson's eyes darted back and forth between Charley and the detective. Mark's rapid-fire questions seemed to disarm him. "As I said, Beanish only coached here."

"But it wasn't that much of a secret that the club was in some financial difficulty," Charley said in a softer tone to try to calm Watson's growing agitation. "My grandmother even knew."

"Some of our suppliers complained that they weren't being paid on time or that the payments were short. That was when *I* brought in a special accountant to look at the books." Watson crossed his arms over his chest and leaned back in his chair, looking smug.

"Do you think he had two ledgers?" Charley asked. "Did the special accountant find any evidence of a second set of books?"

"No, we never found it. But the accountant was able to recreate the transactions. Of course, he could only go back a few years."

"How long do you think it was going on?" Mark asked.

Watson shrugged.

"Carter works with money. He would know how to cover his tracks," Charley said. "How did he lose control of the situation? Did he get greedy or sloppy?"

"That's the question, isn't it?" Watson said. "But it doesn't really matter. The special accountant said even the most recent transgressions would be difficult to prove."

"So, you simply allowed him to resign?"

"For the good of the club. We didn't want a scandal."

"Have you at least informed the bank where he works? If Carter was embezzling from the club, maybe he was doing it elsewhere, too."

"It wasn't our concern. You have to understand, we were trying to protect the club's legacy."

It went against Charley's sense of justice. People who committed a crime needed to be held accountable. She'd exposed corruption when she worked the city beat. If the stakes hadn't been so high, she'd love to unmask Carter, too. But that wasn't why they were here. Watson had given them privileged information to try to help them solve Beanish's murder. She couldn't break the old man's confidence.

Charley blew out a breath in frustration as she and Mark walked back to the car. "Well, so much for that."

"It would have been a little too neat," Mark said. "But if Beanish didn't know about the embezzlement, and the rowing club wasn't going to disclose it anyway, Carter would have no reason to have him killed."

"Or to frame Dan."

A black taxi screeched to a halt on the street, backed up, and then pulled into the rowing club's driveway.

"Mrs. Hall," Romeo Arcadi leaned out of his window and crooked his finger. "You must come with me, now!"

"What's going on?" Charley wrenched open the door to the cab.

"Your grandmother—"

"Is she all right?"

"Yes, yes, she's fine. She sent me to find you. It's your brother..."

"Gran?"

Bessie turned toward Charley and sagged as if a huge weight had been lifted from her shoulders. "Charlotte. Thank goodness you're here."

Charley crossed the hospital room. Her formidable grandmother felt small and fragile in her arms. She stepped back and was shocked by Bessie's pale face and the tears trailing down her cheeks. Charley gently wiped them away and urged her to sit. "What happened?"

Charley glanced at her brother, lying motionless in the bed. His head and left shoulder were bandaged, and there were abrasions on his face, arms and hands. Blood had clotted in his beard and she called to the nurse for a basin of water and a cloth.

"I don't know," Bessie was saying. "They found him in the river, along with that damned sailboat." She sobbed. "He hasn't regained consciousness."

Charley took the cloth from the nurse and gently rubbed away the traces of blood on Freddie's cheek and chin. His skin was sallow grey and his breathing shallow. An intravenous tube extended into his arm, the steady drip-drip-drip of its lifesaving liquid flowing into him. She kissed his brow and whispered a prayer for his recovery.

The nurse had brought in a second chair and Charley sat down beside Bessie, taking her hands. "He's strong."

"Is he?" Gran's question echoed Charley's own concerns. The Freddie who had returned home from the war wasn't the same as the one who had left in '39.

"Do you think he'd been drinking?" It frustrated Charley that Gran didn't seem to take seriously Freddie's obvious problem with alcohol. Charley had hoped, after Freddie's near death a few months ago, that Bessie would support her efforts to convince him to seek treatment—or at least ban alcohol from their home. Instead, she'd continued to turn a blind eye to the situation. Maybe now she'd realize he needed help.

She shook her head. "I don't know," she whispered. "That Corporal MacNamara, from the RCMP, was here earlier. He said he'd be back when...if...when he wakes up."

"Of course, he'll wake up." Charley squeezed Bessie's hand, trying to pass on a reassurance she didn't entirely have.

"I knew there'd be trouble when that sailboat reappeared." Gran's teary-eyed gaze focussed on Freddie. "I had no idea Freddie was going to keep it and try to sail it. Did you?"

Charley withdrew her hands and tucked a loose curl behind her ear. "He said something about that," she admitted. "But I didn't think he'd actually try sailing it on his own."

"You've been so busy with that Beanish murder, you haven't been around much, have you?"

Did Gran mean that as the chastisement it sounded like?

"Dan doesn't have a lot of time before he goes to trial," Charley tried to explain.

"That's why I hired Detective Spadina."

Yes, Gran was definitely reprimanding her.

"I've also been trying to find out where the sailboat has been all these years," Charley said.

"It would be better if we all forgot about the *Lady Stonebridge*," Gran said bitterly. "Hasn't she caused enough devastation to our family?"

"I know it's painful, but can you tell me about it?" Charley knew Freddie's accident was bringing up painful memories of her parents' deaths, but she also sensed that it might prove to be the impetus, finally, for her grandmother to talk about that time.

"You know everything there is to know."

"I don't know anything, Gran!" Charley softened her tone and added, "You've never talked to me about it."

"Well, you were so young. Your grandfather and I tried to shield you from the loss."

"And I appreciate that. More than you can ever know. But now, I would like to learn more. Not how they died but how they lived. I'd like to know who my parents were."

"All right. I guess that's a reasonable request." Gran gave her a sad smile. "Where would you like me to begin?"

"Well, how about the name of their boat. *Lady Stonebridge* seems like a very odd choice for a sailboat."

"Oh dear, you really don't know much about them, do you?" Gran tsked. "The *Lady Stonebridge* was named after your mother."

Charley stood and poured two glasses of water from the pitcher on the table beside the bed. Bessie accepted the glass and took a sip before continuing.

"Your father was a war correspondent and, in 1915, was stationed with the 1st Canadian Division, in France. In April of that year, the Germans launched their first chlorine gas attack on the Western Front. The Canadians were called in to Kitcheners' Wood to counterattack and, as your father phrased it, 'seal the gap' created by the attack." She took another sip of water. "Most of the division didn't make it. Your father was injured—machine gun fire—but he survived and was sent to England to convalesce."

"Which is where he met my mother." This much she already knew.

"Yes." Gran's features softened and she smiled. "Lady Cynthia Pierrepont."

"Lady?"

"Daughter of the Earl of Thorton."

"Wait a minute. Are you saying we are descended from royalty?" Charley glanced toward Freddie. This was just the type of gossip he'd get a kick out of hearing. She couldn't wait to tell him as soon as he woke up.

"A very minor aristocrat, but yes. Like the estates of many noble families during the war, the Earl's became a convalescent home for injured soldiers. Your mother helped as a nurse's aid." Gran reached out a hand and cupped Charley's cheek. "She was such a loving person. And your father absolutely adored her. We all did."

Charley swallowed past the lump in her throat. She didn't often miss her parents—she had no real memory of them so there was nothing to miss—but every now and then, their absence hit hard, and it always caught her off guard. What was she like? What kind of mother would she have been?

Lady Cynthia Pierrepont. Pierre pont...

"Oh, I get it now." Charley sat up. "*Pierre pont* is French for stone bridge."

Gran nodded.

"What happened to my mother's family in England? Why have we never heard from them?"

"The Earl and his wife did not approve of their daughter marrying a commoner, never mind someone from the colonies. They pretty much disowned her. It broke your mother's heart to be estranged from them. We tried to make it up to her, but the pain was always there." She scowled. "And then, after the accident, that horrible woman had the audacity to turn up here and try to claim guardianship for her daughter's children."

Charley had never seen Bessie express a negative opinion of anyone so vehemently. She knew her grandmother held strong and sometimes controversial views, but she kept them to herself. She always urged Charley to do the same.

"I gave her a piece of my mind, let me tell you," Bessie continued. "And we sent her packing—your grandfather and I—back to her country estate in the Midlands. We let her know, in no uncertain terms, that she was not welcome here. She'd given up all rights to you and your brother when she'd treated Cynthia so shabbily."

"Are there more of them?" Charley asked. "How much family do we have in England?"

Gran's lips pursed with displeasure. "I believe Cynthia had a brother, but she never spoke about them after she arrived here. And I think it would be best if you followed suit."

Charley leaned in and kissed Bessie's cheek. "Of course, Gran. You and Freddie are all the family I need." Behind her back she crossed her fingers, knowing full well she was going to learn all she could about her mother's aristocratic family.

"Mrs. Hall?"

Charley jerked awake. She heard and felt her neck crack as she looked up at the nurse who was shaking her gently awake. "Is everything all right?" Charley's eyes flew to the bed, but Freddie was still there. Unconscious.

"There is an RCMP officer here who'd like to speak with you."

"Oh." She stood and stretched, trying to shake off her exhaustion. "Fine. Let him in." She glanced at her watch. It was barely 7 a.m. "And do you think it would be possible to get a coffee?" she asked and immediately regretted her presumption. This was a hospital, not a hotel, and surely the nurse had better things to do than fetch coffee for a family member who'd already defied the rules by staying well past visiting hours.

Charley had insisted Bessie return home to rest, promising she'd call if there was any change in Freddie's condition. The nursing staff hadn't been pleased that Charley intended to stay the night but agreed when it became clear neither she nor Gran would budge.

"Good morning, Mrs. Hall," Corporal MacNamara said as he brushed past her and went directly to Freddie's bedside. "Has he regained consciousness?"

The officer's brusqueness grated on her, but then again, it *was* early. Maybe he needed a coffee, too.

"No, I'm afraid not," Charley said, coming to stand beside him. She glanced down at her brother and her heart ached. She wanted him to wake up, she truly did, but seeing how peacefully he was resting now, she despaired for the return of his demons once he awoke.

"What does the doctor say? Is he going to wake up? And if he does, is he likely to remember anything?"

Charley turned to MacNamara and looked closely at him for the first time. He was taller than she remembered, but perhaps that was because he'd been standing beside Sergeant Bronson who was easily six-foot-four. And he was younger than she'd first thought. Perhaps that accounted for his lack of subtlety. His brown hair was cut very short and he had non-descript, brownish-green eyes. But most striking was how his face appeared to be carved from a block of wood—very square with a notch seemingly cut out of his chin.

"I haven't been able to speak with the doctor yet, but there is no reason to assume he won't wake up. Is there?"

"Just asking, ma'am. When he does, I need to be notified immediately." He started walking toward the door.

"Of course." Charley tucked the blankets around Freddie, feeling suddenly protective of him. "Do you know what happened?"

"Not really." MacNamara paused and massaged the brim of the hat he was holding. "He was found floating near the entrance to the Cataraqui River by a young couple out for a romantic paddle. The sloop was run aground not too far away. The damage is significant."

Charley dearly wanted to ask MacNamara if Freddie had been drinking but couldn't muster the courage. She was sure he had to have been drunk to take the boat out on his own since he knew nothing about sailing. But this was her brother, and she felt the need to protect not only him and but also his reputation.

"In fact," MacNamara continued, "I think the sloop is beyond repair. Probably best to junk it."

Charley closed her eyes in relief. If they got rid of the sailboat, Freddie's screwball plan to become a sailor would be over and he'd be safe. She was sure Gran would agree. "Yes, go ahead. Thank you."

"Very good. I won't disturb you any further, Mrs. Hall. But, please, call me when your brother regains consciousness."

"Wait!" *Darn it!* Getting rid of the boat would be best for everyone, but it had belonged to her parents. It had meaning for her family. Charley shouldn't be the sole arbiter of its fate. "Don't do anything with the boat for now, please. I need to speak with my grandmother first."

MacNamara left just as the nurse returned with a steaming cup of coffee. Charley thanked her and apologized at the same time. Gratefully, she sipped the coffee and returned to her vigil.

It seemed all she ever did these days was worry about Freddie and the effect his drinking was having on their lives. She had managed to save him last time, when his addiction had almost killed him, but what about now? She glanced at her brother. How could she help him when he wouldn't share what was wrong?

Gran arrived several hours later, carrying a picnic basket. "I had Irena make some sandwiches and a thermos of coffee." Her voice was strong and commanding as Charley was used to, but she was pale and had dark circles under her eyes. She put down the basket and went to Freddie's bedside. She brushed her fingers down the side of his head and kissed his cheek. "I asked Mr. Arcadi to wait and take you home so you could rest and freshen up."

"I slept in the chair," Charley said. "I don't need to go home."

"Suit yourself. Has the doctor been by?"

"No, but Corporal MacNamara was here."

"Anything new to report?"

"No." She'd wait until Freddie was on the mend before raising the fate of the *Lady Stonebridge*.

Gran opened the picnic basket and poured herself a cup of coffee from the thermos. Charley declined the offer of some for herself. She'd already downed the coffee the nurse had brought earlier and any more would only make her jittery.

"Well, I intend to wait here until Freddie wakes up," Gran said, taking her seat.

However long that will be.

The morning seemed to drag on. Finally, the doctor arrived, trailed by three young men in white coats. He gave Freddie a cursory examination, explained that there was nothing to be done but wait, and then led his flock of interns on to the next patient.

"I think I am going to get a little fresh air." Charley felt frustrated beyond measure. Waiting wasn't in her nature.

It took her only fifteen minutes to walk from the hospital to the police station. She'd thought about it all night, but in the end, she felt she had no other choice. She had to let Dan know about Freddie and explain why she was going to let Mark finish the investigation alone. They may have their differences, but she trusted Mark would find the truth. He may not believe it, but Charley knew that truth would exonerate Dan.

As she mounted the steps from Market Street, she was almost bowled over by Marillo and Adams.

"Hey, wait!" she called after them.

"No time to talk," Marillo called back and the two disappeared around the corner of the building.

"What's going—?" Charley stopped dead on the threshold to the building at the sight of Mark Spadina leaning casually against the information counter in the lobby. "What are you doing here? Has there been a break in the case?"

"A good morning to you, too, Mrs. Hall." He straightened. "And yes, quite possibly."

"Why don't you wait in the Sergeant's Office," Sergeant Kearn said from behind the counter. "This could take a while."

Charley followed Mark into the now-familiar office. "What's going on? What do you know?"

"I had a hunch," he shrugged. "And it may have paid off."

"Are you going to tell me?"

Mark left the door ajar and motioned for her to sit. Once she did, he perched himself on the corner of the desk and faced her. "I was tipped off by a pawnbroker that he may have come into possession of some items belonging to the Beanishes."

"A pawnbroker? How would he even know?"

"When you hired me, I reached out to the re-sale community and asked them to keep their eyes open for anything that might belong to a rower."

"Why would you even think to do that? There was no report of anything being stolen?"

"Motive." He shrugged. "It's usually the husband or

wife. But if it's not, it's generally the help, and the motive is often robbery."

"What do you think was stolen?"

"I was told that a pair of gold cufflinks, engraved with the Frontenac Rowing Club's insignia, was being pawned, along with a pair of diamond earrings."

"And you think it was someone in the Beanish household?"

Mark gazed out from under his dark, hooded eyes. "That surprises you?"

"I guess it does. It never occurred to me to consider..."

"Let me ask you, Charley, how much do you know about the people who work for you?"

"What do you mean?"

"Well, for example, your former maid, Chantal. Do you know where she was from? How old she was? Where she is now?"

"No, but what does that—"

"What about Irena? Have you ever had a conversation with her that wasn't about what to serve for dinner or when to clean the family silver?"

"I don't think I like what you're implying."

"I'm not implying anything. I am clearly stating that you and your kind give about as much thought to the people who serve you as you do to the furniture you sit upon."

"My kind? You make us sound no better than slave owners. We take care of the people who work for us. We pay them a good wage for their service." *How dare he!* "How well do *you* know any of them?"

Mark's smile didn't extend to his eyes. "Chantal Beauchemin was born and grew up in Trois Rivières," he began. "She was twenty years old when she came to Kingston to try to earn enough money to help her family. She is now back home, helping her widowed sister care for her two young children as well as their aging mother. Irena Nowak immigrated from Poland with her sister-in-law after the war. Her husband was a soldier in the Wojsko Polskie. He was captured by the Nazis and died in a forced labour camp."

Charley slumped in her chair. "How did you find all this out?"

"I asked. People appreciate when others take an interest in them." He shrugged. "Frankly, I'm surprised. For a reporter, you show a remarkable lack of curiosity about the people around you—at least, those not of your ilk."

Charley felt as if she'd been sucker-punched. He couldn't be right, could he?

But she didn't know any of the information he'd conveyed about Chantal and Irena.

Maybe he made it up?

No, she was quite certain he hadn't.

Charley had always thought of herself as a kind, caring person. She would have vehemently denied that she was classist, and yet it had never occurred to her to have an actual conversation with Chantal, Irena, or any of the other housekeepers and governesses they'd employed over the years.

She felt nauseous. This wasn't who she thought she was. But then, she'd also just learned her mother was the daughter of an earl. So, what did that make her?

It was starting to be all too much for her. She tucked the Pierrepont information away to deal with later.

And as for Mark's assertions, well, he was simply wrong. Chantal and Irena may have felt comfortable talking about themselves with Mark, but Charley doubted they would have felt the same with her. There was a certain protocol that family and staff followed. It was a shorthand that made sure everyone knew what was expected of them. Mark didn't understand that good help is meant to be invisible.

But how invisible?

Was it possible that in her bias she'd overlooked a potential suspect in Frank Beanish's murder?

"Aha." Mark stood as a commotion arose outside the door. "The good constables are back. Maybe now we'll get some answers."

"SPADINA WAS RIGHT," Constable Marillo said, placing the small objects in a tray on the top of the information counter. "Mrs. Beanish confirmed these objects belong to her and her husband."

"That's good work." Sergeant Kearn nodded at Mark. "I'm not sure we would have thought to look at pawn shops all the way over in Amherstview."

"Lucky break," Mark said with uncharacteristic modesty. "I just happened to learn that the maid had family there."

And how had he done that?

Charley stomped down her irritation. It was their first big break. She should be appreciative.

"Adams went to get us a couple of sandwiches. He should be back any moment then we'll go pick her up," Marillo said.

"You didn't spot him a fiver for it, did you?" Kearn asked.

"Of course I did. That kid never has any money on him."

"Or he plays you for a sucker." Kearn chuckled and returned to cataloguing the jewellery.

"Do you really think the housekeeper could be the

murderer?" Charley asked the constable. She desperately hoped this lead would help free Dan, but it still didn't make a lot of sense to her. "That Frank Beanish was killed over a few pieces of jewellery?"

Marillo raised two fingers to his cap in a brief salute and walked away but not before Charley caught the look he threw at Mark, as if to say, "she's your problem." Kearn's head was studiously cast down.

"People have been killed for less," Mark said.

"But Beanish was killed in his boathouse. These items would have been taken from the main house. And besides, I thought the killer had to have been a man."

"Look, Charley. There are a lot of things we don't know yet. Likely, she had a male accomplice. Women usually do. At the very least, the maid is a thief. But maybe she knows more. Where was she when Beanish was murdered? Why wasn't she around when the police tried, initially, to interview her right after the murder and then when they returned the next day?"

"Well, I assume since it was Dominion Day, she had the day off, like most domestic staff. And as for why she wasn't around when the police went back, Georgia said she'd sent her home. That she wanted to be alone."

"Georgia?" Mark took a step closer to her, his eyes darkened menacingly. "You've spoken with the widow? You're on a first-name basis?"

Too late, Charley realized she should have kept that piece of information to herself.

"I went with Gran. It was a social call."

"Your grandmother knows her?" Mark stalked around the foyer like a caged lion. "I've been trying to talk to the widow for days, but she won't see me. And now, you tell me your grandmother, *my client*, could have arranged a meeting?"

"I'm not sure she would have done that," Charley said. It gave her a small sense of satisfaction to know she wasn't the only one Gran liked to keep secrets from. "It wouldn't be proper to harass the poor woman while she's grieving."

"She's a suspect, Charley!"

"I don't think she did it," Charley said. "She seemed genuinely—"

"Unbelievable!" Mark threw up his hands and glared at her. "You need to take me to see her."

Charley hesitated. It was hard not to feel like she was competing with Mark to solve the case. Besides, hadn't she come here to tell Dan she couldn't help anymore? Still, with this latest development, she found herself being drawn back in. Freddie was unconscious and there was nothing she could do for him until he woke up.

"You want to exonerate the good alderman?" he growled. "You take me to the widow."

"Fine. I will make arrangements." She saw Mark's eyes dart down to her hands, checking to make sure she hadn't crossed her fingers, a tell he'd figured out when they'd last worked together.

She hadn't. What would be the point?

"Hey Jerry," she called to the sergeant, anxious to be rid of Mark. "Since we're waiting around, do you think I could see Alderman Cannon?"

"Sure. I'll bring him to the office."

"Charley!" Dan's face brightened with pleasure when he saw her. He shuffled toward her, the shackles scraping along the floor. Then he saw who was lounging against the wall. "What's he doing here?"

Mark straightened and walked to the centre of the

room, stopping inches from Dan. "I'm here to save your hide, Sport."

"And how is a disgraced cop going to do that?" Dan stepped even closer. "Frankly, I'm surprised they even let you in the building."

"At least I know they'll let me out."

The two men glared at each other. Dan had a couple of inches on the detective but unencumbered by chains, Mark had the advantage.

"Stop it!" Charley said, inserting herself between them. "Mark, if you can't be civil, you can leave." She turned to Dan. "Gran hired him to help prove your innocence."

"No, let's be clear, Mrs. Hall. Your grandmother hired me to find the killer. I'm still not convinced the police haven't already got their man," Mark said. "I have to say, Sport, prison agrees with you. I don't think I've ever seen you looking better." He didn't even try to dodge Dan's attempt to punch him. The shackles ensured Dan's fist barely raised above his waist, stopping well short of its mark.

Charley's slap, on the other hand, hit Mark's unsuspecting cheek with a loud thwack. He staggered backward and then rounded on her, fists raised to attack before he caught himself and lowered them. "I guess I deserved that."

She couldn't read his expression, but her own heart was racing with fear. His reaction had been swift and automatic. She knew if he hadn't quickly regained his composure, she would have been in real trouble—even with the sergeant standing a few feet away. Mark wasn't like most men she knew. He was dark and dangerous. The predator in him always lurked below the surface. She'd do well to remember that.

Mark stalked out into the lobby and Jerry took his seat behind his desk.

Charley looked up at Dan and her heart clenched. His cheekbones had become more prominent in the few days since she'd last seen him, while his whiskey-brown eyes seemed to have sunk deeper into his face. He was still snappily dressed, but his trousers hung looser on his hips and the white shirt wasn't quite so crisp.

"My hero," Dan said.

"It's not funny. I don't know why the two of you can't get along." She turned away from him and sat down in the nearest chair. If he only knew who Mark really was.

"I just don't like him." Dan took the second chair.

Charley sighed. The fact they shared a mother, which neither had ever known, probably wouldn't make the slightest bit of difference to Dan. It certainly didn't to Mark.

"Can I ask you something?" Charley said. Mark's comments about her "kind" still grated on her. "How much do you know about your mother's housekeeper?"

"That's an odd question," he said warily.

"Is it? Why?"

Dan closed his eyes and inhaled deeply. Then he leaned in closer and spoke in hushed tones. "My mother would be mortified if she knew I was telling you this. So please, keep it to yourself."

"Of course."

"We no longer have a live-in housekeeper like your grandmother does—haven't had for a few months. I don't know if you've noticed the last few times you've been over, but my mother answers her own door and pours her own tea."

Charley was taken aback. Now that he mentioned it, she didn't remember seeing any household staff when she'd visited Rose. "Are you saying your mother does everything? The cooking and the cleaning?"

"Oh, heaven's no. Could you imagine?" Dan chuckled. "No, we have a woman—Louisa—who comes every day to clean, shop and prepare meals. But she doesn't work weekends and she doesn't live with us. Each evening, she goes home to Bayridge, to her husband and kids—two, a boy and a girl." He lowered his voice even further. "The shipbuilding industry hasn't been doing so well since the war. We've done our best to transition to peacetime activities, but..." He shrugged. "That's why my father is in Europe. He's trying to secure more contracts."

"You told me things were slow, but I had no idea," Charley said. "I'm sorry."

"Don't be." He leaned back and attempted to cross his arms only to be thwarted by the shackles. "We recovered after the last war; we will this time, too."

She admired Dan's optimism. At the same time, it surprised her how much he knew about Louisa—far more than she knew about anyone who'd worked for Gran.

Maybe Mark was right. Her privileged station and upbringing had blinded her to others around her. It was an unsettling realization.

"Have you spoken with Donnelly?" Dan's voice brought her back to the moment.

He looked so hopeful, she hated herself for even considering abandoning her investigation into Beanish's murder. Dan was already carrying an enormous burden—not only facing the murder charge but also dealing with the financial troubles of his family's company. She wouldn't add to them.

"I haven't been able to find him, yet. But I promise you, I'll keep looking."

Dan, her lifelong friend and confidant, needed her. She wouldn't let him down.

"WELL, IT'S ABOUT TIME!" Bessie rose from her chair as Charley entered Freddie's hospital room. Then, noticing Detective Spadina right behind her, she muttered, "I might have known."

"How is he?" Charley crossed to the bed where Freddie lay. His colour was better than it had been that morning, but there were creases of worry around his eyes and a tension between his brows.

His eyes flew open. "Boo!"

"Ack!" She jumped back, then glared down at her brother, impossibly annoyed and immeasurably relieved at the same time.

"Sorry, couldn't resist," he said, struggling to sit up higher in the bed.

"He regained consciousness a couple of hours ago," Gran said.

Charley helped Freddie adjust his pillows. Although he was awake, she could tell by his slow, calculated movements that he was still in a lot of pain. "What did the doctor say?" she asked, turning back to the room. "Oh, hello Laine, I didn't see you there."

Laine approached the bed and handed Freddie a glass of water. "He still needs a lot of rest."

"But he'll be all right, won't he?"

"We think so."

Charley didn't think that sounded as promising as it should. She turned back to Freddie. "What happened?"

"I don't know."

"Do you remember going out on the sailboat, the *Lady Stonebridge*?"

Freddie shook his head and winced.

"Corporal MacNamara was here, again, but Freddie couldn't tell him anything," Gran said.

"MacNamara?" Freddie asked. "Who's that?"

"You remember, one of the RCMP officers who came to the house to tell us about finding the *Lady Stonebridge*," Charley said. "He came by first thing this morning and said to let him know when you woke up. I guess one of the nurses must have contacted him."

Laine had stepped back so Bessie could stand beside the bed.

"I don't remember talking with anyone from the RCMP or going sailing on...what did you call it? *Lady Stonebridge*? Why would I do that? I don't even know how to sail."

Gran raised her head and gazed at Charley across the bed. Her eyes flickered with fear.

Charley swallowed the lump in her throat and patted her brother's arm. "Don't worry about it. You just work on getting well." She strolled out to the hallway where Laine was chatting quietly with Mark. "Is this typical?" she whispered. "I mean I've heard of people forgetting traumatic incidents, but he can't seem to remember anything about the boat prior to the accident."

"There is so much we don't know about brain injuries," Laine said. "At least he recognizes you and your grandmother. He even knows me. So that tells me his long-term memories are intact."

"But he doesn't remember meeting Corporal MacNamara or going down to the docks to see the *Lady Stonebridge* —that was Friday, last week. And he forgot that he spoke to Corporal MacNamara only a few hours ago."

Laine shrugged, a helpless expression clouded her eyes.

"What is the last thing he remembers? Do you know?"

"Yes, we asked. He doesn't seem to have any memories after coming home from a baseball game on Dominion Day."

"He doesn't remember going out drinking with his mates afterward?" Charley asked.

"I don't know. We didn't know what he'd done after the game, so we couldn't ask for specifics. We only know what he told us was the last thing he remembered doing, and that was coming home and changing out of wet clothes. And talking to you and your grandmother about the rowing club tea."

"You think he was drinking when he took out the sailboat," Mark said. It wasn't a question.

"I do," Charley said miserably. "But I also can't help wondering if this isn't the first time he's lost his memory. Maybe the reason he hasn't told us about what happened to him in the war is because he's forgotten."

"No," Mark said with certainty. "If he was lucky enough to have forgotten, he wouldn't be drinking."

Charley watched her grandmother help Freddie lie back down. "When he wakes up later, will he remember I was here?" Charley asked.

"I don't know," Laine said. "All we can do is wait for his brain to heal itself."

"So, Detective," Gran said, joining them, "can I assume you are here to give me an update on the progress of our case?"

"There are a few leads, but I will wait until I have something more substantive before reporting them to you."

"And the other matter I stipulated?" She glanced meaningfully at Charley.

"Unfortunately, that has not gone according to plan," Mark said.

"Indeed."

Mark's face reddened and he glanced down at his feet like an embarrassed schoolboy. Charley was inordinately pleased to see how Gran's one-word reprimand had chastened him. But when he looked up, his dark scowl was aimed directly at her, and her heart pounded uneasily.

"Oh Charley, good. I was hoping I'd find you here."

Charley turned to see Grace walking along the hallway, grateful for the distraction. Then she threw a nervous glance at Gran before turning back to the *Trib*'s archivist. "Why are you here?"

"Hello everyone." Grace ignored Charley's question. "Mrs. Stormont. Detective." She turned to Laine. "How is Freddie?"

"As well as can be expected," Laine said.

"I'll say a prayer for him."

"That would be very much appreciated, Miss Fletcher," Gran said. "I'm going back inside."

"Have you found out anything?" Charley asked in a hushed voice.

Mark took a step closer. "Is this about Beanish?"

"No, it's about the *Lady Stonebridge*," Grace said.

"What did you find?"

"Not much. I can't find an official report of the investigation into your parents' deaths, but I did speak with a New York State police officer who remembers the case."

"After twenty-five years?"

"Yes. He was new on the job and it was the first time he'd ever seen a dead body."

"That experience often leaves a marked impression," Mark said, chuckling.

"Indeed, Detective, but it was more than that. This officer was an experienced sailor; I guess he had crewed in college. He felt there was something off about the accident." Grace opened her notebook. "Let me get it precisely. The rigging was overtight."

"What does that mean?" Charley asked.

"Simply put, the purpose of the rigging is to secure the mast's position," Grace said. "If the mast is too far forward or backward, it will lead to poor handling."

"In that case, wouldn't you want the rigging to be tight?"

"You would think so," Laine said. "But you actually want your rigging to be a bit on the looser side, as loose as possible while still holding the mast in position."

"You see, if the rigging is too tight, the mast hasn't got any give and it could snap in a strong wind," Grace added.

"In this case, though, the mast didn't snap off, did it?" Charley was sure that detail would have been important enough to report on.

"No, you're right," Grace admitted.

"Still, a poorly rigged boat *would* affect its handling," Laine said.

"The officer I spoke with thought it was odd given that your father was an experienced sailor, and the incident occurred on the *return* trip. But he was very junior in the investigation and there was nothing that could be proven conclusively." Grace flipped her notebook closed. "And as for the sloop, he says if it wasn't claimed by the family it likely ended up sold or in drydock."

"Well, that's interesting but it doesn't tell us much." Charley turned to glance through the windowpane of the door to Freddie's room. Bessie was sitting, holding Freddie's hand.

"No, I'm afraid it doesn't." Grace moved closer to Charley and followed her gaze. "How is your grandmother doing? It must be devastating for her, first to have the *Lady Stonebridge* mysteriously reappear and then for Freddie to be..."

"I don't know how she does it." Charley watched her grandmother's lips moving in a silent prayer. "Her inner strength has been the glue holding our family together after my parents' deaths, and then Grandpa. And when we thought Freddie had died in the war..." She swallowed past the lump in her throat. "I don't know how much more she can take."

"You'd be surprised how resilient people can be," Mark said in a surprisingly kind tone.

"That's very true," Laine chimed in, reassuringly placing her hand on Charley's arm. "We see it in medicine all the time."

"Thank you for trying anyway, Grace," Charley said. It was all so frustrating. Charley felt she was being stymied at every turn. If Freddie couldn't remember what happened, would this be yet another mystery that remained unsolved?

"I hate to be the bearer of more bad news," Grace said, "but I don't have any information on the J. Donnelly front, either."

"Who's J. Donnelly?" Mark asked, his dark eyes back to their usual intensity.

"Someone Dan suggested might have had a motive to kill Beanish," Charley supplied. "I've tried calling the only J. Donnelly in the city directory several times, but there's no answer. I even went around to his house a couple of times, but he never seems to be home."

"Are you talking about Jacob Donnelly?" Laine asked.

"Dan said his name was Jake or Jack. He hasn't seen him since his rowing days at Queen's and he couldn't remember. Why? Do you know him?"

"Late twenties?"

"That would be about right."

"If it's the same fellow, he's up on the fourth floor, in our veterans wing."

"Oh." Charley couldn't hide her disappointment. The veterans wing housed many of the soldiers who'd returned to Canada but could never truly go home. Their injuries, whether physical or mental, were so severe they were incapable of rejoining society.

Another dead end.

"He's not a permanent patient," Laine said as if reading Charley's mind. "He's definitely emotionally scarred from the war, but most of the time he's able to live a fairly normal life. He comes in and out of here whenever he feels the demons have become too difficult to bear—or when someone else does."

"When did he arrive this time?"

Laine cocked her head and bit the side of her cheek for a moment. "Of course," she said, smiling at her recall. "It was last Thursday night. Dominion Day. The fireworks often trigger terrible memories for the vets. I was working in

Emergency when his friend brought him in because he was acting erratically. He was concerned Jacob would harm himself or someone else."

"Thursday?" Mark snapped. "We need to see him. Now."

CHARLEY PACED AROUND THE VISITORS' room. She wasn't good at waiting. Laine had said she'd see if Donnelly would talk with them, but she wouldn't force him. The decision would be entirely his.

Mark, on the other hand, was patiently seated in one of the wooden chairs, eyes closed and appearing as if he had all the time in the world. She'd filled him in on the history between Donnelly, Beanish and Dan. He'd agreed that it was hard to discern a motive for Donnelly to want to frame Dan, but the timing of his commitment to the hospital was suspicious.

"How can you just sit there so calmly?" Charley's irritation got the better of her. She always considered Mark a man of action, poised to strike even when he was seated.

"My dear Mrs. Hall," he drawled, keeping his eyes closed, "don't you know that fifty per cent of police work is waiting? Waiting to process a piece of evidence. Waiting to speak to a witness. Waiting for a suspect to make a mistake. If I allowed myself to become as agitated as you, I am sure I would be in the loony bin by now."

At the sound of the doorknob turning, Mark's eyes popped open and his body tensed; in an instant, the predator was back.

Laine led a young man to one of the wooden chairs. He completely dwarfed her; even sitting down he was almost as tall as she was standing. When she introduced Charley and Mark, Donnelly kept his head bowed, his body slumped. The trousers of the dark blue pajamas he wore were too short for his long legs, and the left sleeve of the pajama top that should have encased his arm was, instead, empty and tacked to his shirt.

"I'll sit over here," Laine said, placing a reassuring arm on Donnelly's shoulder. He didn't respond.

Charley muffled her disappointment and tried to open the conversation. "I understand you used to be a rower?"

Donnelly gave no recognition he'd even heard her. She looked to Mark. Was there any point in continuing this? Whatever reason Dan may have to be suspicious of Donnelly was irrelevant. There was no way this one-armed man could have wielded the oar that killed Beanish.

"You were with the Fifth Armoured." Mark pointed to a maroon-coloured swatch of cloth that had been sewn onto Donnelly's sleeve. "I recognize the patch."

Donnelly stirred, but kept his head bowed.

"That was no duck soup. Is it true they shipped you to Italy without your own vehicles and expected you to make do with leftovers from the Desert Rats?"

Donnelly looked up.

"I was with the 48th Highlanders. Saw some action in Italy," Mark continued.

Mark was in the war?

Charley knew it shouldn't come as a surprise given his age, but he'd never mentioned it. Then again, he'd always shown great insight whenever they discussed Freddie's demons. Maybe his understanding came from battling demons of his own.

"Yeah, it was FUBAR," Donnelly said. His voice was rough and raspy, as though he hadn't used it in a long while. He cleared his throat. "What they gave us was either from North Africa or a two-wheel drive, neither worth shit in Italy." He glanced back at Laine. "Excuse my language, ma'am."

"Where'd you leave your gun?" Mark asked.

Donnelly glanced down to where his left arm should have been. "Ortona."

"I remember. We were on the western ridge, outside town."

Donnelly looked up. "Then you don't really know what it was like."

"No," Mark conceded. "I've only heard stories."

Donnelly sat up straighter in his chair. "Why are you here?"

"I want to ask you about Dan Cannon."

Donnelly looked back at Laine with alarm. "I didn't mean it. You know I wasn't right in the head at the time."

Charley and Mark exchanged surprised glances. Maybe Dan was right? Maybe there was a reason to suspect Donnelly?

"Shhh." Laine came to stand beside him. "You're safe here."

Charley didn't know how Laine could make that promise, but then again, if Donnelly wasn't right in the head when he had done whatever it was he'd alluded to, then he'd probably end up at Rockwood Asylum rather than Kingston Penitentiary anyway.

Mark threaded his fingers behind his head and leaned back in his chair, deceptively appearing relaxed. "We're only here to talk, Jake. What was it you didn't mean to do?"

"The letter," Donnelly said.

"You sent Cannon a letter?" Mark's voice was nonchalant. "What's wrong with that? I am sure the alderman gets letters all the time."

Donnelly licked his lips and glanced nervously at Laine. "Well, it wasn't a very nice letter. I said some things I shouldn't have."

"Did you threaten him?"

"I might have."

"Well, you know what you wrote, don't you?"

"Yeah, okay, I threatened him."

"Did you threaten to kill him or just hurt him?"

"Kill him."

"Can I ask why?"

"Well, he ruined my life, didn't he?"

Charley was mesmerized by Mark's cool handling of Donnelly. His actions and the tone of his voice were all meant to make the young man comfortable enough to confide in them. And it was working. She'd never seen this side of the detective before. It impressed her as much as it irritated her. She was certain Donnelly would never have opened up to her. Heck, he had barely even acknowledged her presence.

"Are you talking about when you were at university?" Mark asked. "I thought he sought justice for what happened to you."

"He should have left well enough alone." Donnelly's voice was bitter. "I'd left the team. I didn't ask him to do anything about it."

"You didn't want anyone punished for what happened to you?"

Donnelly shook his head. "It was embarrassing enough that it happened, but only the team knew about it. It would have all blown over—been forgotten—by the next term if he hadn't pushed for the coach to be fired."

"But he did."

"Yeah, and so then the whole campus knew what happened to me."

"That must have been hard."

"He made me look like a sissy. I dropped out. Tried to find work but couldn't. I signed up as soon as the war started." He thrust his left shoulder forward to emphasize the missing arm. "And this is the thanks I got."

"So, you wrote Cannon a letter threatening to kill him. Is that all you did? Did you ever contact your former coach, Frank Beanish?"

Donnelly's gaze shifted back and forth between Mark and Laine. "No, why would I contact him? He's as much a victim of this whole mess as I am."

"What do you mean by that? That he's a victim?"

"Well, he lost his job, didn't he? I heard he had to leave the country to find work."

"Did you know he was back?"

"No. I don't have anything to do with any of those rowers anymore."

"Did you hear he was dead? Murdered?"

Donnelly's eyes bugged out of his chalk-white face.

"And that your old pal Dan Cannon was found standing over the body and has been charged with his murder?"

"I... I..." Donnelly's mouth opened and closed like a landed large-mouth bass.

"We think he's being framed," Mark said smoothly.

"Not by me!" Donnelly leapt to his feet. "I didn't—I wouldn't kill anyone." His head swivelled around, frantically looking for an escape.

"But your letter...?"

Laine placed a reassuring hand on Donnelly's good shoulder and gently guided him back to his seat.

Charley glared at Mark. "There is a huge difference between writing a threatening letter and actually carrying out a violent act," she said in a low voice. "I told you how Beanish was killed. Look at him. Do you honestly think he is capable of that?"

Mark held up his hands to surrender to her point. "I don't think he, himself, killed Beanish, but he did have it in for the alderman. Maybe he knows more than he's letting on."

"I don't!" Donnelly shouted, clearly having heard Mark's supposition. "It was a stupid letter, written when I was feeling sorry for myself, that's all."

"Where were you the afternoon of Thursday, July first?" Mark ignored the death-stare Laine threw at him. "For the record."

"I was with friends at a baseball game. It was called on account of rain. Then we went to the waterfront..." He lowered his head into his hands. "That's the last I remember until Sunday past."

Wasn't Freddie at the same game?

Charley shook her head. That was irrelevant. Half the city was there, according to the report she'd read. But it was a strange coincidence that the baseball game was the last thing both men remembered.

"Fireworks," Laine said. "I explained that to you already." She patted Donnelly on his back. "It's okay, Jacob," she said to him in a soothing tone. "Let me take you back to your room."

Charley watched Laine gently help Donnelly to his feet.

She felt a twinge of guilt at the look the doctor gave them as she led her patient from the room. Disapproval. But what had Laine expected? They were trying to solve a murder.

"Do you really think he was involved in Beanish's murder?" Charley asked Mark.

Mark stood and straightened the crease of his pants. "Not a chance."

"Then why imply he did?"

"To see his reaction. Until then, I couldn't be sure."

"Even though he only has one arm?"

"As with Mrs. Beanish or her maid, it was entirely possible he could have been working with someone."

Charley stood up slowly. "At least now we know why Dan thought he might be a suspect."

"Ah, yes, not his biggest fan. I am surprised, however, that your alderman didn't tell you about the death threat."

"He's not— Oh, never mind." What was the point? Mark was hardly a fan of Dan, himself. And he did have a point, darn it! Why hadn't Dan told her about the death threat?

She pushed away her frustration and changed the topic. "Speaking of the housekeeper, let's go back to the station to see if the police have anything more." With any luck, the felonious housekeeper will have confessed to having an accomplice who'd killed Beanish, and Dan would be set free before the start of his trial tomorrow.

"It's getting late," Mark said, taking her arm and guiding her out into the hallway. "Your grandmother was looking pretty frail. Now that you know Freddie is out of the woods, I suggest you take her home and you both get a good night's sleep."

"But—"

"I'll go to the station and I'll call you if there is any news."

"Okay," she reluctantly agreed. She was feeling tired and achy thanks to the uncomfortable hospital chair she'd slept in. The thought of a hot bath was tempting. "But you will call me if you hear anything. Promise?"

"Pinky swear." Mark held up his hand with his baby finger extended.

She shook her head at his foolishness. The man was a mystery.

"I didn't know you fought in the war," she said as they rode the elevator down to Freddie's floor.

"Who said I did?"

"You did. To Donnelly."

Mark leaned back and crossed his arms. "Let me ask you something, Tiger: Are you always perfectly honest when you interview someone for a story you're working on?"

"Are you saying you made it up? That you didn't serve in the 48th Highlanders?" She stepped out of the elevator, but he didn't follow her. She turned back just in time to see the doors glide closed.

Sure, she sometimes let people think she was interviewing them about something other than what she was truly after. She'd done it with Robin Carter only yesterday.

But when he'd been speaking with Donnelly, a shadow had come over Mark. It was the same shadow she saw in Freddie whenever she tried to get him to talk about his war experiences.

If Mark hadn't served, how had he known the 48th's position during the battle for Ortona?

And if he had, why deny it?

CHARLEY FEARED she had reached a dead end.

The next morning was spent in jury selection, after which the judge ordered a brief, late-morning recess. The Crown prosecutor would then make his opening arguments followed by a longer lunch break.

Dan, smartly dressed in a light-weight brown suit and tie, had sat stoically through the entire proceeding, his eyes on the pool of prospective jurors. The goal was to appear respectable and respectful to counter the Crown's plan to portray him as a crazed killer bent on revenge. He scanned the gallery as they were leading him away for the break, his gaze seeking and finding both Charley and Rose. He flashed them a warm smile and a brief nod. It only made Charley more frustrated—she needed a breakthrough.

Charley pushed her way out of the courtroom, purposefully avoiding her press colleagues—especially Lester Pyne, who kept pestering her for special access to Dan. The fact the trial was proceeding, combined with the lack of a telephone call from Mark last evening, seemed to indicate that the Beanish housekeeper was another dead end. Still, she wanted to confirm that for herself.

She had intended to stop by the *Trib* before heading to the courthouse this morning, but she'd given in to the luxury of sleeping in. By the time she'd gone down for breakfast, Gran had already left for the hospital to visit Freddie—Charley would go over the noon hour—so she'd poured herself a cup of coffee and wandered down to the kitchen were Irena was washing dishes.

Mark's criticism still rankled.

Despite Charley's best attempt, Irena was reticent to talk about herself. How did Mark do it? He certainly didn't seem to be the type of person anyone would feel comfortable opening up to. And yet, she had watched him bring Donnelly out of his shell yesterday, and he had obviously managed to do the same with both Irena and Chantal.

She'd always thought of herself as a great interviewer. She'd gotten people to spill the beans on all sorts of things they hadn't wanted to. But that was for the paper. This was different. This was personal.

"Mrs. Hall!"

Charley slowed her pace and glanced back to see Mark hurrying along the sidewalk.

"I thought I'd find you here," he said when he caught up to her.

"I was on my way to the police station to see if they have any news."

"I can save you a trip. The housekeeper was indeed working with a male accomplice, but they both have airtight alibis for the day Beanish was killed."

Charley slowed her pace. "Okay, so now what?"

"Was the widow in the courtroom?"

"No." Georgia's absence hadn't surprised Charley. What wife would want to listen to the details of her husband's grisly murder?

"Then I think we should pay her a visit."

"We can't suddenly drop in on her unannounced."

Charley stopped walking and turned to him. She could only imagine Gran's reaction to such a suggestion.

"Then give her a call. I am sure she'd appreciate some company today, while all this is going on."

"This would hardly be a social visit," Charley said, incredulously.

"Just call her."

"Fine." She scanned the street for the nearest telephone booth. "But while I do, you need to go to the market and buy flowers and some cinnamon cakes. We are not going empty-handed." The gesture was unlikely to appease Gran, but it made Charley feel better.

Georgia had sounded pleased at the prospect of a visit on the telephone and seemed genuinely welcoming when they arrived. Charley introduced Mark as a friend, not mentioning that he was a private detective.

"I couldn't bring myself to go to the courthouse," Georgia said as she placed the flowers in a vase. "Is that awful of me?"

"No, of course not. The wheels of justice will roll on whether you are there or not," Mark said smoothly.

"Will they expect you to be a witness?" Charley asked.

"The Crown prosecutor said that likely wouldn't be necessary. He seems to think he'll get a conviction before the weekend." She gave a weary sigh. "It is all so awful. Not only Frank's murder but then to learn that our housekeeper was stealing from us. I've never had a housekeeper before. Is it common for staff to steal from you?"

"No." Charley ignored Mark's raised eyebrows. She knew his opinion on the matter. "We've never had anything stolen."

"Well, I guess every bushel has one bad apple."

"Was anything else taken?" Charley asked.

"No. I went through the house and everything seems to be in its place. The problem is, the police want me to check the boathouse, too." She swallowed heavily. "I haven't been there since..." She shook her head. "I don't know that I can do it."

"Would you like us to go with you?"

"Would you? I would be so appreciative."

Charley tried to hide her excitement as she glanced at Mark. This was a better outcome than they could have hoped for. And yet, guilt hovered over her like a rain cloud. Were they taking advantage of Georgia's distress? Mark still considered her a suspect.

Charley had only ever seen the boathouse from the rowing club across the river. Up close, it seemed more like a home that nudged up against the water's edge.

"The boathouse was the reason Frank wanted to rent this property," Georgia said, unlocking the door. "He was hoping old Mrs. Foster would eventually sell it to him."

The land side of the boathouse consisted of a large, open room that seemed to serve as a kitchen and office. Cupboards and a counter lined one wall. A rough wooden table with two chairs completed the eating area. Against the opposite wall was a wooden desk, a tall filing cabinet and bookshelves. At the far end was a window and a door leading out to a three-sided room, open to the water.

Charley peered through the window and spied an old canoe turned upside-down on the floor and rows of various types of paddles and oars hanging on the wall.

It had happened out there. That was where Frank Beanish had been attacked and killed.

"The police said they cleaned everything up," Georgia said remaining near the land side entrance. "But I can't look."

"I can't see anything," Charley said.

"I'll go check to make sure," Mark said.

"Oh, Mr. Spadina, if you would. I would be ever so grateful."

Charley wandered over to the office area. Was it normal for a desk to be so pristine? She thought of her own desk at the *Trib*, covered with scraps of notepaper and file folders containing story ideas. "He was very tidy," she said.

"Oh yes. Very particular. Everything had its place."

Charley turned to the bookshelves. One long shelf, at eye level, held several trophies of different shapes and sizes, but there was a gap. She looked closer. A thin layer of dust covered the shelf everywhere except there. "What was here?"

Georgia came to Charley's side. "Oh dear," she said. "Not the cup. That was his pride and joy." She glanced around the room. "I can't imagine where it would have gone."

"Was it valuable? Do you think your housekeeper and her accomplice may have taken it?"

"I'm not sure how valuable it was, but it seems to me if they were looking to steal something, they would have taken the medals." She pointed to two medals hanging from a hook below where the missing trophy should have been. "They're gold-coated."

Charley recognized the medals from the photograph she'd seen at the rowing club the other day. "The trophy, was it the Ontario Cup?"

"Yes, yes." Georgia took down a photo and handed it to her. "Here is a picture of Frank and your father when they won it."

Charley gazed down at the familiar photo. "I think you should call the police."

Mark returned while Georgia was on the telephone. "Nothing." He sounded disappointed.

Charley filled him in on the missing trophy.

"That's personal," he said. "Especially if they didn't take the more valuable medals. Someone wanted that trophy for themselves."

"Well, Dan certainly didn't have the trophy on him when he was arrested," Charley whispered to him, before returning the photograph to the shelf where another framed picture caught her eye. Two young couples—her parents, Frank Beanish and another young woman, probably his first wife—standing on the deck of a sailboat.

"Your parents," Georgia said, coming up behind her. "Frank never forgave himself for their deaths. It haunted him for as long as I knew him."

Charley picked up the photograph. "What could he have done? It was an accident."

"He and Aggie were supposed to go that day, but she was pregnant and wasn't feeling up to it. Frank always thought that if he had been there, he could have stopped whatever happened."

Charley allowed herself a moment to wonder what her life would have been like if Frank and Aggie had gone with her parents, if he had been able to stop the accident, if her parents hadn't died that day. Then she shook off the fanciful thoughts. Dreaming about what might have been was never a worthwhile pursuit. And in all likelihood, there would have been four deaths to mourn.

"He found her, you know," Georgia said.

"Who?"

"The *Lady Stonebridge*."

Charley's heart stopped and she whirled to face Georgia. "*He's* the one who found her? He brought her here?"

"It was like an obsession when he came back to Kingston. He'd leave every chance he got to search through the drydocks and yachting clubs all along the New York shoreline. About a month ago he found her, brought her back here, and began making her seaworthy again. He repainted the name on her stern last week."

"Why did he want to find her after all these years?"

Georgia shook her head. "He always said there was more to the accident than what the police investigation concluded."

"But after so long, there would be no evidence on the boat," Mark said.

"It was important to him, that's all I know." Georgia looked down at the floor and sighed. "He was a wonderful man, but I could never share his passion for boats. Rowboats, sailboats, anything that floated on the water. That was what he lived for."

"The *Lady Stonebridge* must have slipped its mooring during the sudden rainstorm on Dominion Day," Charley said. One mystery solved. At least now she knew where it had come from.

"Oh no, it was gone before that," Georgia said. "It wasn't here when I returned home from my appointment, around noon. I told the police that."

"Wait a minute!" Charley's breath rushed out of her lungs. "It was the *sloop,* not the *scull* that was missing?"

Georgia shrugged. "Sloop? Scull? I don't know the difference. It was a boat, and it's still missing."

PRECISION. *Precision. Precision.*

How often had Dan drilled that into her head?

Scull. Sloop. Sweep.

She hadn't thought it mattered, but it did. It mattered greatly.

"What are you thinking?" Mark asked as he backed his car out of the Beanish's driveway.

"I'm thinking the police are relying on faulty information in establishing their timeline. What if Beanish was in the boathouse the whole time Georgia thought he'd gone out on the sloop? It's entirely possible he was killed earlier in the day, long before Dan ever arrived. Remember what Laine said about there being too many variables that could have interfered with the onset and duration of *rigor mortis*."

"What about the *Lady Stonebridge*? Did the murderer take it deliberately or did it simply break free from its mooring?" Mark asked.

"Frank Beanish was an able sailor. Violent storm or not, I don't believe the sloop simply slipped free of her mooring. He wouldn't be that careless in tying her up. Not after all the effort he'd gone to in order to find her. The missing boat has to be connected to the murder."

"Not necessarily."

"But if it is, maybe Freddie's accident wasn't an accident at all."

And maybe he hadn't been drinking.

Charley desperately wanted that to be true but feared it was too much to hope for.

"Well, if we're going to play the 'what if' game, why not take it a bit further? What if your parents' deaths weren't an accident, either?"

Charley leaned back in the seat and closed her eyes, remembering what the New York cop had told Grace about the rigging.

What if?

"We need to see the sloop," she said suddenly. Maybe the *Lady Stonebridge* was finally ready to give up some of her secrets.

"That's where I'm heading."

SERGEANT BRONSON EYED MARK skeptically as Charley explained their reason for wanting to examine the sailboat. He'd said he knew Mark by reputation only when she'd introduced him, and it was obvious his impression wasn't all that favourable. Mark seemed to take it all in stride, appearing unaffected by the officer's scrutiny.

"You're lucky you arrived when you did. We were just about to ship her off," Bronson said.

"Where?"

"Message was you no longer wanted her, so we were going to sell her for scrap."

"But I told Corporal MacNamara I needed to talk to my grandmother and brother before making any decision on that."

Bronson shrugged. "I guess our wires got crossed. Anyway, follow me, I'll take you to her."

The *Lady Stonebridge* was lying on the shore, open and exposed.

"I thought you might have put a tarp on her or something to protect her from the elements," Charley said.

"Why? Until you showed up, she was headed for the scrap heap."

Charley approached the sloop. She didn't know what she was looking for. Something—anything—that seemed out of place. "The damage isn't as significant as I thought it would be."

"No?" Bronson trailed her as she walked around the vessel examining the gaping hole in the hull.

"But it's not so bad she couldn't be repaired," Charley pressed.

"I'm not the expert, you'd have to talk to Mac about that."

"He said she wasn't salvageable, but it doesn't look like that to me."

"When did you speak to Mac?" Bronson's head cocked in surprise.

"When he came to the hospital to check on Freddie."

"Oh, I hadn't realized he'd done that."

"He was there at least twice. No, wait. Three times."

"That's Mac for you. He's a stickler for detail," Bronson said. "And how is your brother?"

"Conscious."

"Good. I'll swing around later today and see if he can shed any light on what happened."

Charley glanced at Mark. With a subtle shake of his head, he told her to keep quiet. Something was off.

"How much of what we're seeing now is the result of

the most recent accident," Mark said, returning the conversation to the boat.

"It's hard to know for sure what sort of shape she was in before Mr. Stormont took her out," Bronson said.

"But you had her here for a week before that," Charley said.

"Yes." Bronson sighed heavily. "But, again, we didn't examine her in any detail. We had no reason to. We were simply looking for the owner of a missing sloop—which we found."

"Ignoring human error for the moment, what would cause a boat to run aground?" Mark asked.

Bronson scratched his head. "I'm not an expert, but I have been involved in a few of these investigations. It could be the current. Could be visibility. Speed. Age of the vessel."

"Aside from age and possible prior damage, are any of those things likely in this case?"

The sergeant shook his head. "Nah. According to the weather station, it was a clear day and the wind wasn't excessive. I suppose it's possible the sloop wasn't entirely seaworthy, but..." He glanced at Charley, then turned back to Mark and lowered his voice. "Frankly, Mr. Spadina, it was most likely sailor inexperience."

"What would it take for another boat to force her aground?" Mark asked.

"I assume you'd be looking at a motorboat. But it was broad daylight. Wouldn't someone have seen something?"

"I never assume anything, Sergeant," Mark countered.

Charley stifled a smile as she moved to examine the boat more closely. "This is broken," she said, pointing to the wooden structure sticking out from the bottom of the boat.

"That's the keel," Bronson said. "That and the rudder were damaged when she hit the shallows."

Charley nodded and pointed to the long slash in the hull. "And that?"

"She must have been running pretty fast when she hit the rocks. It runs down the whole side."

"Can we turn her over?"

"Not easily," Bronson said. "What are you looking for?"

"Proof that someone forced Freddie onto the rocks."

Bronson shrugged. "With Mr. Spadina's help, we can probably lift her so you can have a look."

Mark nodded and he and the sergeant hefted the boat.

Charley crouched down and then crawled underneath the raised boat. "Not a lot of damage on this side," she called out. Her eyes landed on something. "Wait!" She inched her way down the length of the hull.

"Any time now, Mrs. Hall," Bronson grunted.

"I'm coming." She backed out from under the boat and stood up, holding out her thumbnail. "See this? Red paint. I scraped a bit of it off the hull."

Mark and Bronson carefully lowered the boat and examined her thumb.

"It looks like something scraped the side of the boat," Charley said.

"It doesn't necessarily mean someone deliberately ran her aground," Bronson said.

"No, but if we could get a better look at the other side," Charley insisted. "I think there was some damage to the hull as if she'd been rammed."

Bronson's eyebrows arched. "You think so? I'll get some of the boys to give me a hand and we'll get her turned over." He stepped between Charley and the boat. "Until we prove this one way or another, the *Lady Stonebridge* is now a possible crime scene and you have to leave."

"But—" Charley began.

"We'll leave it in your good hands, Sergeant," Mark said, taking Charley's arm and steering her away. "We've done all we can here," he said to her. "Let them do their job."

Charley fumed as Mark slammed the passenger door closed and walked around to his side of the vehicle.

"If you think I'm going to go home and wait around for the RCMP to tell me what they've found, you've got another thing coming," she said when he slid in beside her.

"Woah, Tiger, who said anything about waiting around? Step one was to see if it was possible the *Lady Stonebridge* was relevant in any way to the murder. We don't have conclusive proof she was, but we do have possible proof that her disappearance during the murder and subsequent grounding are not simply coincidences."

"What's step two?"

Mark turned the key and the car's engine revved to life. "What else is missing from the murder scene?"

Charley grimaced. How could she have forgotten? "The trophy."

"Exactly. And why that trophy rather than the more valuable medals that were hanging there?"

"Because it was important to whoever took it."

"Right again. So, let's go visit our friend Boomer, and see who else, in 1914, believed they deserved to win the Ontario Cup."

"OH, Mrs. Hall. Detective. I was just locking up. I need to get home to the missus. She gets quite annoyed if I'm late for tea." Boomer Watson was locking the door when Charley and Mark arrived at the rowing club.

"Please. This is important," Charley implored the club secretary.

"All right. All right. A few minutes won't hurt." He turned and led them back through the club to his office.

Charley took a seat in the office and, as before, Mark remained standing near the door.

"I am interested in learning more about the 1914 Ontario Cup. I gather it was quite a significant win for my father and Frank Beanish," Charley said.

"Oh yes, quite dramatic." Boomer pointed to the cardboard box containing copies of the book documenting the history of the rowing club. "It's all in there. Did you read it?"

Panic tightened her chest. What had she done with the book? It must still be in Freddie's hospital room.

"I haven't had the pleasure," Mark said, covering for Charley. "Can you summarize it for us?"

"Yes, well, it was the largest rowing event in the province, as you might infer from the name. That year, 1914, it was especially important because our club was hosting the regatta. It was also the last Ontario Cup ever held, but of course, we weren't aware of it at the time."

"Because of the war?" Charley asked.

"Yes. In many ways, that year's Ontario Cup signaled the end of an era."

"What about after the war?"

Boomer sighed. "It wasn't the same. We'd lost so many men. No one seemed to have the heart to revive it. Many smaller regattas were held instead, but nothing with the scale and prestige of the Ontario Cup."

"Were Fred and Frank expected to win or were there serious rivals?" Mark asked.

"In straight pairs? It was a large class, if I remember." He pointed to the book. "It's all in there."

"For Detective Spadina's sake, I am sure it will be much more interesting to hear it from you," Charley said. "Were Frontenac's Fabulous Phenoms expected to win their class?"

Boomer sat up straighter, looking very pleased with the request. "No, not at all. They weren't given that name until after their win at the Ontario Cup."

"Who was their main competition?" Mark asked.

Boomer cocked his head and leaned back in his chair. "Well, I hadn't thought about it in a while, but it's interesting you should be asking me about the Cup, given the last time you were here you were asking about the same man."

"Robin Carter?" Charley glanced back at Mark who seemed equally surprised.

"Yes, Carter rowed straight pairs, too. He and his partner were a little older than your father and Frank—

maybe a couple of years. Up until that summer, they'd been the top straight pair for the club, and one of the top three in the province."

"So, the win by Fred and Frank was an upset?" Mark asked.

"I would say so."

"Can you tell us what happened?"

"It was a straight two-mile course. The morning started out windy and with scattered showers, causing some of the competitors to race their heats in the rain. But by the time the finals were held, in the afternoon, the sky had cleared, although the winds remained high. Both teams had won their heats quite handily, and the club was thrilled to have two teams in the final."

As Boomer warmed to his subject, his voice rose in volume, reminding Charley of why he'd been given the nickname.

"It was a great race. Probably one of the greatest I've ever seen. The two teams pulled away from the pack very early—500 yards maybe—and then stayed neck-and-neck right until not more than ten feet from the finish—and even then there was some controversy about the result."

"Why is that?" Charley sat on the edge of her seat. She was breathless and her heart raced as if she was watching the race alongside of Boomer.

"Stormont and Beanish won by a nose—two judges confirmed it. But Carter and Riley complained that the wind whipped up at the last moment causing one of them to miss a stroke and giving an advantage to the other team."

"Isn't the weather and how crews adapt to it part of the race?" Mark asked.

"Of course it is. The complaint was viewed as bad form and wasn't taken seriously."

"But Carter never got over the loss," Charley said.

Boomer shook his head. "As I said, it was the last Ontario Cup. There was no opportunity for a rematch."

"And was he still bitter after the war?" Charley asked.

"Everything had changed after the war. Only Beanish continued to make rowing his life's work. Riley was killed at Passchendaele. Such a loss. Left behind a lovely young *fiancée*..." Boomer's cheeks turned pink. "Oh well, that's not important, is it? Carter became a bank manager and your father had his career as a journalist and started a family. They both kept involved with the club, and both were directors for many years before..." He shook his head and looked down nervously.

"Before what? Charley didn't understand his reticence.

"Oh, dear." Boomer looked distressed. "It was all so long ago. Maybe you don't know. Your father was about to take over as president when..."

"Oh." Charley felt as if she'd been punched in the gut. She hadn't expected so many reminders of her father's life to have an impact on her. "When he drowned," she finished for him.

"Yes. I'm so sorry, my dear. This must dredge up very painful memories for you."

"On the contrary. I don't remember him at all, so I feel lucky to be able to learn a little of what he was like from someone who knew him."

"He was very well-liked and respected in the rowing community. And he would have made a wonderful president."

"After Stormont died, Carter became president and kept his role as treasurer all these years," Mark summarized. "And now you've learned he's been embezzling from the club, but you don't know for how long."

"Yes." Boomer looked miserable.

Charley glanced back at Mark. Was he thinking the same thing she was?

"Thank you, Boomer. You've been most helpful." Charley stood. She couldn't get out of there fast enough.

"WHERE'S THE FIRE, TIGER?" Mark grabbed Charley's arm as they exited the rowing club.

"We've got to go to the police. We have to tell them about Carter." She shook off Mark's hand.

"Tell them what? All we have is coincidence and speculation. We have no proof."

"But the *Lady Stonebridge*, the Cup, the embezzlement. It's all linked to Carter. He killed Beanish. You know he did." She started walking again. "I can't let Dan spend another night in jail for a crime he didn't commit."

"You'll be laughed out of the police station if you go there now," Mark called after her. "So what if Carter was bitter about losing the Ontario Cup? So what if he was embezzling from the rowing club? So what if Beanish had discovered the boat your parents were on when they drowned? Stop and think, Charley. You're a reporter. Would you publish the story based on such flimsy evidence?"

She hesitated. He was making sense, darn him anyway. She opened the car door. "Then let's go through what we do know and figure out what more we need."

"Now you're talking."

She waited until Mark had pulled out onto the main

street before she spoke. She'd been cataloguing the information in her head, laying it out as if she was preparing to write an article. "Here is what we know. First, there was bad blood between Carter and my father because of the Ontario Cup race. Second, my father was about to become president of the rowing club, a club Carter was treasurer of. Third, my father, a lifelong sailor and strong swimmer, drowns while sailing under what everyone acknowledges were ideal conditions."

"Freak accidents happen all the time. Maybe your mother fell overboard, and he tried to save her."

"Whose side are you on here?" Charley frowned.

"I'm playing devil's advocate. The drowning only becomes relevant if it wasn't a drowning at all but a murder, and that it was perpetrated by Robin Carter."

"Boomer said there was no way of knowing how long Carter had been embezzling from the club. What if he'd been doing it all along? What if my father found out?"

"Even if he hadn't found out, as president there was a good chance he would—especially given their contentious relationship, and the fact your father was a journalist and therefore prone to asking questions."

"Therefore, Carter kills him and takes over as president. Everything is fine for over twenty-five years. Then Beanish returns from England and becomes involved in the rowing club again." Charley paused. "This is where things get murky. What happened to make him kill Beanish? It couldn't have been the embezzlement. Boomer swore he didn't know about it."

"It's the boat. It has to be."

The sloop. The Lady Stonebridge.

"Georgia said Beanish had just repainted the name on the stern," Charley said. "But after so many years, there would be no proof that Carter had killed my parents, would there?"

"Unlikely," Mark said. "But would he know that?"

"Maybe seeing the boat unnerved him and he confronted Beanish. Killed him. Took the Cup, which he always thought should have belonged to him, and...what? Sailed off in the *Lady Stonebridge*?"

"If he thought the boat was going to connect him to the murder of your parents, he might have taken it away, hidden it somewhere, with the intention of destroying it in the future."

"And then we had that sudden violent storm and it got loose on the river. He must have seen it when Freddie took it out and he tried, again, to destroy it." Her stomach lurched. "He killed my parents and tried to kill my brother!"

"But he didn't succeed," Mark said. "Freddie is going to be fine."

She wasn't so sure, but that was an entirely different conversation.

"Hey, wait a minute," she said. "What are we doing here?" Mark had turned into the driveway to her home.

"It's late. There's nothing else we can do today." He turned off the engine.

"No! I'm not stopping now." She whirled to face him. "Not when we're so close to solving this."

"Look, Tiger, I appreciate your enthusiasm, but we're a long way from solving this thing. A good night's sleep will do us both some good."

"And what about Dan? How good is his sleep going to be?" She flopped back against the seat and crossed her arms.

How did Dan fit into this? Was he simply a convenient

scapegoat for the murder? She still didn't have the answer to that one.

Mark heaved a sigh. "What do you suggest?"

"I want to go to Carter's house."

"He's not going to let you into his home."

"Let's at least see if he owns a red motorboat and go from there."

"I HATE DAYLIGHT SAVING TIME," Mark muttered as he followed Charley along the brush edging Carter's property, down to the waterfront.

Charley glanced back. It was 7 p.m. and still bright as midday. The sun wouldn't set for almost two hours.

While Mark had waited in the car, she'd gone into the *Tribune*'s offices where Grace had helped her locate Carter's address. Fortunately, Pyne and Sherman had left for the day, so she hadn't had to face either of them.

She'd been glad to learn Carter had a waterfront home. That made it all the more likely he'd have the motorboat on his property—she was sure she was right about him owning one. Otherwise, she'd have had to track it down at any number of marinas in the area.

Carter's property wasn't nearly as grand as the one Beanish had rented. There was a small dock but no boathouse. A covered rack held a rowing scull and canoe. And there, floating in the water, was a bright red motorboat.

"Gotcha!" Charley whispered.

"Not quite," Mark said, stopping beside her.

"Let's go closer to see if there's any damage from ramming Freddie," Charley said.

"You're not likely to see anything as long as she's in the

water. And if you do manage to find something, how are you going to know if it's from ramming Freddie or from ramming a dock?" he said but followed her anyway.

Mark was right. It was hard to tell if the boat had sustained any damage as it bobbed up and down, knocking against the dock with each gentle wave.

"I need to speak with him," Charley said.

"Carter? Are you out of your mind? Why would he talk to you?"

"I don't know, but I need to try." She started across the backyard toward the house.

Mark hurried past her and stood in front of her forcing her to stop.

"Get out of my way!"

"Listen, Charley, the man is dangerous and devious. It's time to call the police."

"You were right before. We don't have enough evidence," she said.

"What do you hope to accomplish by confronting him?"

"If he has the Ontario Cup, we can place him in the boathouse."

"And then?"

"And then, maybe, I can use that information to get him to confess to killing Beanish and framing Dan."

"Is that all you want?" Mark asked with unexpected perception.

"No. You're right. I want him to confess to killing my parents." There, she'd admitted it. She knew there would never be enough evidence to take to trial, but she desperately wanted Carter to take responsibility for what he'd done—how he'd changed her life and Freddie's forever.

Mark's features softened and he expelled a long breath. "All right, Tiger, give it a try. We don't want to spook him, so I'll wait outside. But if I hear anything or think this thing's going sideways, I'll be in like a shot."

"Thank you."

Charley rounded the house and mounted the front steps onto the porch. She raised her hand to knock but as her fist touched the wood, the door glided open.

"Hello?" she called, leaning into the foyer. "Mr. Carter? Are you there?"

Nothing.

"It's Charley Hall. I'd like to speak to you."

Silence.

As she stepped over the threshold, she could smell the sickly-sweet odor of cigar smoke and followed it down a short hallway to a half-opened door.

"Mr. Carter?" she called again before entering the room where a familiar coppery smell mingled with the tobacco.

Blood.

Carter was sitting in a chair, slumped forward, his face down on his desk.

Charley approached slowly, noting the half-empty brandy snifter sitting in a growing puddle of blood oozing from the man's head. But that wasn't what caught her attention. Rather, her focus was on the large trophy on the other side of the desk. "Ontario Cup. 1914," she read out loud. She reached out her hand—

"Don't touch anything!"

She whirled around at the command and froze at the sight of two handguns trained on her. She raised her hands slowly.

Constable Marillo lowered his weapon. It took Adams a few moments more before he followed suit. Charley could see Mark standing in the doorway behind them.

Adams walked past her to examine the body. He

crouched down to get a closer look at the victim's face. "It's Carter," he said, rising.

"Take Spadina and make sure the house is secure, then update dispatch," Marillo said.

"What? He's not one of us!" Adams said.

"No, but 'one of us' needs to stay with the body and the other has to make sure the murderer isn't still in the house." Marillo frowned. "Now, I would suggest that Spadina here —disgraced cop and all—is still a safer option than doing it on your own. But maybe that's just me."

Adams scowled at the rebuke. "Fine." He brushed past Spadina. "Let's go."

Marillo shook his head and sighed before turning to face Charley. "Now, Mrs. Hall," he said, sounding aggrieved, "what are you doing here?"

"I'm following a lead," Charley said. "You?"

"Same."

"So, you *are* still investigating the Beanish murder. You know Dan—Alderman Cannon—is innocent, don't you?"

"I know nothing of the sort," Marillo said. "We are here because earlier this evening Mr. Carter called the station and said he had some information about a crime that had been committed some years ago."

Was Carter calling to admit to the embezzlement? "Did he say what it was?"

"No. He would only talk in person, not over the phone."

Mark returned to the doorway. "There's no one in the house. Your partner's updating dispatch now."

"Thank you," Marillo said.

"Am I under arrest?" Charley asked.

Marillo's eyes widened in surprise. "For what?"

"Murder. You found me standing over a dead body.

Shouldn't you charge me with murder? That's what you did to Alderman Cannon. Why should this be any different?"

"Aye yai yai." Mark threw up his hands in exasperation.

Marillo grinned and turned to him. "She with you?"

"Yeah, I'm afraid so." Mark crossed the room to look more closely at Carter's body.

"How was he killed?" Marillo asked.

"Single gunshot to the back of the head," Mark said. "The slug's probably still in the desk."

"So not self-inflicted?"

"Not a chance."

Marillo turned to Charley "Do you have a gun on you, Mrs. Hall?" he asked with exaggerated patience.

"No, but I could have disposed of it. And I'm sure the detective has one that I could have used."

Mark nodded, withdrew his pistol and held it up, sniffing the barrel. "I do, but as you can see, it hasn't been fired." He returned it to its holster.

Charley scowled at him and rounded on Marillo. "I'm just saying you arrested Alderman Cannon with no evidence other than his presence at the crime scene."

"And clothes covered with blood indicating proximity to the victim, not to mention access to the murder weapon, *and* a substantial motive." Marillo held up his hands in appeasement. "Look, Mrs. Hall, if you truly want to help the alderman, tell me why you are here."

A revving engine echoed off the water.

Charley glanced at Mark in panic. "The motorboat," they said in unison.

"What? Wait!" Marillo called out as they raced past him, out the front door, and around to the backyard, crossing the lawn to the dock.

"It's gone," Charley said, as the red speck disappeared around a bend in the river.

Mark's response was a more colourful expletive, for which he immediately apologized.

"All right, you two," Marillo said, breathing heavily. "You'd better tell me what's going on."

It was well after midnight when Mark dropped her off at the entrance to the Kingston General Hospital. He'd tried to convince her to go home to sleep, but she hadn't seen Freddie all day and her mind was whirling from everything that had happened. Sleep was a long way away.

Even though they'd interviewed her and Mark separately, she was confident their stories would be consistent, providing the information necessary to convince them of Dan's innocence.

Except it hadn't.

The police maintained that everything she had told them was circumstantial. Even Carter's possession of the missing Ontario Cup wasn't strong enough. Georgia couldn't confirm it had been in the boathouse the morning of the murder. The boathouse was her husband's sanctuary which she rarely entered. The cup could have been taken days before or even given to Carter by Beanish himself.

The embezzlement, too, had been dismissed. "It's a long way from stealing money to bashing someone's brains in with a paddle," Adams said, relishing a little too much in his gruesome description of the murder.

And as for a connection between Carter, Freddie's grounding, and her parents' deaths? Well, that hadn't even warranted a rebuttal. Marillo and Adams had simply ended the interview and wished her a good evening.

But taken all together... Why couldn't they see it?

At this point, the police were confident they had Beanish's murderer locked behind bars. Their focus was solely on finding Carter's killer.

Charley ignored the disapproving glares as she passed the nurses' station on her way to Freddie's room. She'd broken the rules before—what was one time more?

Carter was the key to solving this whole thing. She was certain of it. But he was dead. Someone had wanted to silence him. But why? Was it because he was going to confess to the police?

No, that's not what Marillo had said. He'd said Carter told them he had *information about a crime that had been committed some years ago.*

"There you are." Freddie looked up from the book he was reading as she entered the room. "I thought you'd forgotten about me."

"Never." She kissed his forehead. "I thought you'd be asleep. How are you feeling?"

"Pretty good. The headache's almost gone, but my shoulder is still sore."

"Have you been able to remember anything about the accident?" Charley asked, perching herself on the edge of the bed.

"Some of it's coming back to me—not the accident itself, unfortunately—but other things around that time."

"I'm sorry, but I need to ask you something and I really need you to be honest with me. It's important." Charley swallowed heavily. She'd thought about this, tried to look at it from all the angles, but in the end, she'd been ready to write off Freddie's accident as his fault. "I originally blamed you for your accident. I assumed you'd been drinking and that was why it happened. So, I am asking you now, were you drunk at the time?"

"I don't think so, no," Freddie said slowly. He frowned and rubbed the stubble on his chin. "No, I am quite sure I wasn't."

"I am sorry, but I had to ask."

Freddie wrapped his arms around her and pulled her head to his chest. "It's not like I haven't given you cause for thinking that," he said. "I know you worry about me."

"I wish I could do something to help you. To make things better for you." She pushed against his chest and looked up at him. He seemed so vulnerable. It was sometimes hard to remember he was the older sibling.

"Don't give up on me."

"Never!" She leaned against him and listened to his heartbeat. "But no more sailing, please."

"I can't promise that," Freddie said. "As soon as I can get the *Lady Stonebridge* back, I intend to make her seaworthy again."

She sat up, speechless. Surely, he wasn't serious.

"Laine and Grace have promised to teach me. It will be perfect. They know how to sail but don't have a sailboat. I've got a sloop but don't know how to sail her."

"But why? That boat has brought us nothing but heartache."

"Kind of like me." Freddie smiled down at her. "In all seriousness, though, I am hoping the water and fresh air will be precisely what is needed to redeem both me and the *Lady Stonebridge*."

FREDDIE HAD FINALLY FALLEN ASLEEP. Charley wished she could do the same. She was still too much on edge. The book Boomer Watson had given her lay on the windowsill. Maybe the *History of the Frontenac Rowing Club* could help her pass the time.

She quickly flipped past the inscribed page, cringing at the sentiment, '*May the Stormont tradition continue...*' Freddie's determination to pursue sailing didn't sit well with her. She had a few choice words for her two friends the next time she saw them.

She paused at the photographs of the first board of directors. She rarely saw pictures of her grandfather as a young man. He was tall, towering a good three-to-four inches above the rest of the group. *President*, she read. An honest one, unlike the club's most recent chief.

She was tempted to linger over Frederick I's rowing exploits but decided to save that for another time—maybe with Gran, once she'd proven Dan innocent.

It turned out, there was a whole section about the 1914 Ontario Cup—not only the various heats, but the significance of the event itself. She skimmed it, but there was nothing in addition to what Boomer had already told her and Mark.

She read through the boxed section that commemorated Scott Riley, Carter's rowing partner who'd died at Passchendaele, and savoured the pictures of her father, and occasionally her mother, in various rowing activities after the war. Another box highlighted a tribute to her parents after their deaths in 1923.

As she scanned more of the photographs, she noted how many were of Frank Beanish, not only standing proudly behind teams of the young rowers he coached, but also with his wife, Aggie, and their daughter, Cynthia—named after

Charley's mother. It was bittersweet to see the young girl growing up within the pages of the book, knowing that she was destined to die before her fifteenth birthday.

There were many of photos of Boomer Watson. She smiled at the conceit—well, why not? It was his book, after all. And of course, as club president for so many years, Robin Carter made an appearance in more than his fair share of photos, too.

Hmmm, that was odd. Was Carter married? He never seemed to be photographed with a woman, as his other contemporaries were. She went back through the book and took more careful note of his photos. No, not a woman, but throughout the book, beginning around 1919, when he returned from the war, Carter was often pictured with a young boy—no name given in the cutlines. Charley flipped through the pages, watching the boy age from around five years old to perhaps twenty, the round cherub face slowly molding into what, in adulthood, resembled a square block of wood with a notch in his chin.

"WHAT IN HEAVEN's name happened here!"

Charley's head snapped up and her heart leapt into her throat. It took her several seconds to remember she was in the *Trib*'s morgue—had been since she'd seen the photographs of Corporal MacNamara in Boomer Watson's book. She looked up at Grace and smiled sheepishly. "Sorry, I must have dozed off."

The *Trib*'s archivist tut-tutted as she surveyed the damage Charley had done to her normally impeccably organized room. Documents were spilling out of open filing cabinet drawers, old copies of the *Tribune* had been dragged out of storage and lay scattered on the large worktable surrounding a haphazard pile of old city directories. "How long have you been here?" she asked.

Charley looked at her watch. *Eight-fifteen.* "About five hours, I guess." She stood and stretched. "I need a coffee." She paused at the door. "I'll be back to explain and help you clean up the mess."

"I should hope so."

Charley generally avoided the newsroom coffee. One could never be sure how old it was or how strong. Today, though, she'd have to chance it.

"Oh, Mrs. Hall, you're here." Lester Pyne was hanging his hat on the coat rack near his desk.

"Yes, I work here," she snapped.

He giggled. "I've caught another murder," he said, almost too gleefully. "Another rower, if you can imagine."

"Who'd have thought rowing was such a dangerous pursuit?" She picked up one of the mugs beside the coffee maker and inspected it.

Clean enough, I guess.

She filled the cup, sniffed its contents.

Better question: is it coffee?

Pyne took a mug and filled it without hesitation. She watched in horror as he added four scoops of sugar and a big scoop of powdered milk and began stirring wildly.

That is definitely not coffee!

"Robin Carter," Pyne said. "I've got to write it up quick so I can get to the courthouse for the Cannon trial at ten."

Charley was on the verge of suggesting he might want to pursue whether there was a connection between two dead rowers in as many weeks but stopped herself. Pyne's lack of inquisitiveness was the reason she was so confident she'd get her old city reporter job back.

"I'm sorry about the mess, Grace," Charley said when she returned to the morgue.

"What was so important that you couldn't wait until I got here?"

"I couldn't sleep so I came here."

"Hmmm. I'll be having nightmares about what you've done to my room for weeks." Grace propped herself up on one of the stools. "What is it that you're looking for?"

"A birth notice for a baby boy named MacNamara." Charley motioned to the old *Kingston Tribune* newspapers on the worktable. "It should be around 1914 to 1916. But I can't find anything."

"Birth notices cost money. Not everyone can afford it. Plus, Kingston has two newspapers. It could be in the *Whig-Standard*."

"Plus, I am not even certain he was born in Kingston."

"Oh Charley, then searching for a birth notice is likely the worst way to find someone."

"So, what would you suggest?"

"Well, you've pulled out all my city directories—is he there?"

"No."

"Do you know when he was in Kingston for certain? Could there be school records?"

"Possibly."

Grace jumped down from her perch and rustled through a mound of file folders. "It's funny you mention that name. Where is it? Yes, here." She held up a file. "An Alice MacNamara died in Rockwood Asylum Wednesday night. I remembered the name because my cousin married a MacNamara. They're not related. I checked."

"What did she die of?"

Grace shook her head. "It just says 'lungs.' I get the death notices from Rockwood in case they relate back to any stories we've done. But as far as I could tell, Alice MacNamara never appeared in the *Trib*."

"How old was she? Did she have a son?"

Grace looked down at the paper. "She was 52. It doesn't mention any family."

"So, she *could* have had a son. Is there any way to find out what she did? Anything more about her?"

"I can do some digging, but why is she important?"

"I am looking for a connection between an RCMP officer named MacNamara and Robin Carter."

"The dead guy?"

"You know about that?" Charley was surprised.

"I ran into Pyne on the way in. He was positively bursting to tell me he had another murder to report on." Grace narrowed her gaze. "The question is, how did you know about it?"

Charley lowered her voice. "Okay, don't tell Pyne, but I discovered the body."

"Oh, my heavens, Charley! What have you gotten yourself into now?"

"I think his murder is related to Beanish's."

"And you think this MacNamara is involved somehow?"

"Possibly."

"Does this MacNamara have a name?"

"Corporal." Charley shrugged. "That's what I am trying to find. His superiors only referred to him as Mac. Once I know who he is, I'm hoping I can figure out his connection to Carter."

Charley flipped open Boomer's book to the image of Carter and MacNamara that she'd flagged and showed it to Grace.

"Do you think Carter is his father?" Grace asked the obvious question.

"I don't know. I went looking through old *Tribs* to see if Carter had a wife. If the boy wasn't his own, perhaps he married someone who already had a child. But what I found was a 1920 marriage notice for Robin Carter and Laura Simms—not MacNamara. The boy would have been around five-years-old."

"Well, he must have been important to Carter," Grace said, flipping through the book. "He's in most of his photos."

"Oh, I'm such a ninny," Charley said, lightly slapping her forehead. "I know who probably knows."

"Boomer Watson?" Grace grinned.

"You're way ahead of me, as usual."

"Maybe if you had a good night's sleep once in a while, you'd catch up."

Boomer answered the telephone on the second ring.

"I was reading your book last evening and noticed that most of the board members are pictured with their wives, but Robin Carter never is. There is a boy, however..." Charley paused and waited but Boomer didn't respond. "It's just, he's not identified in any of the photos. Is he Carter's son?"

She could hear Boomer draw a deep breath and exhale slowly. "No, the son of a very good friend, that's all."

"Why wasn't he ever named?"

"Mrs. Hall, you know I don't like to gossip. Some things are better left alone."

"I'm afraid I can't. Robin Carter was killed last night."

"What? Oh dear. Oh dearie, dearie dear."

"I need to know who the boy was."

"To notify him?" Boomer asked.

"Yes," Charley said, crossing her fingers.

"Off the record, all right? I don't want to be spreading stories."

"About Carter?"

"No, no, no. Robin Carter stepped up and went far beyond for that boy and his mother. It cost him his marriage, most likely."

"What was the boy's name?"

"MacNamara. We called him Mac."

Charley blew out a frustrated breath. "His *first* name?"

"You're not going to publish this, promise?"

"I promise."

"Riley. Riley MacNamara."

"As in Scott Riley? Carter's old rowing partner?"

"Now you know why we called him Mac and why I didn't publish his name in my book," Boomer said defensively.

"Scott Riley died in Passchendaele, and you did mention to me that he left behind a *fiancée*. Are you saying he left behind a son, too?"

"To be fair, I don't think either of them knew she was pregnant before he shipped out. I would like to think if he had known, he would have married the girl right away."

"But he didn't. And he died. And because they weren't married, she wasn't entitled to any compensation from the government."

"Oh, it was far worse than that," Boomer said. "Allie was from a well-respected family. They disowned her, cut her off completely. And Riley's family wouldn't acknowledge the boy, either. If Carter hadn't stepped up to help, they would have been completely destitute."

"What happened to them?"

"I don't know. I never kept up with her, and Mac stopped coming around the rowing club years ago. How did Carter die, by the way?"

"I'm sorry, Boomer, I'm not at liberty to say." She was running out of fingers to cross. "But thank you. You have been most helpful."

Charley chewed on the end of the pencil she'd been taking notes with. Was there anything here? Could it simply be coincidence that Corporal MacNamara was put on the case of finding the owner of the *Lady Stonebridge*, the boat Carter had taken after killing Beanish? Or was he more involved, perhaps helping to cover up the murder in order to save the man who had done so much for him and his mother?

It was a damning accusation to make toward a member of the federal police force. Charley would have to tread carefully.

She glanced at her watch. It was almost ten o'clock. Dan's trial was about to resume. She should be there for him, especially since everyone presumed today would be the final day, and a verdict was expected to follow shortly afterward.

She'd have to work quickly if she was going to clear Dan before that happened. She dialed the number Romeo Arcadi had given her.

Let's see what Corporal Riley MacNamara has to say.

"Corporal Riley MacNamara?" Charley pushed open the door to the room she'd been directed to in the RCMP's Kingston detachment.

MacNamara looked up from the typewriter. "Mrs. Hall." He stood. "This is a surprise. Are you here about the sloop? Or do you have news about your brother?"

"A bit of both," Charley said. She'd worked on several possible scenarios during the drive over. MacNamara had been insistent she report on any changes in her brother's memory so she could use that if he was reluctant to see her. And, she'd use the sloop as an excuse to talk with MacNamara, rather than Bronson. In the end, neither had been necessary. She'd asked to speak with him at the front desk and the officer had simply directed her.

"Please, have a seat." He indicated a chair and returned to his own seat behind the desk. "I am trying to catch up on a bunch of reports. It's slow going, though. I am a poor typist."

"I'm sorry about your mother," Charley said. It was a guess, but she had a hunch that Riley's Allie and the recently deceased Alice were one and the same. From his startled and then suspicious reaction, it was a good guess.

His face hardened and he eyed her suspiciously. "How do you know about my mother?"

"Oh, we get all kinds of reports at the *Trib*. She was at Rockwood Asylum, but the report said she died of a lung condition."

"My mother wasn't crazy if that's what you're getting at."

"I wasn't suggesting anything of the kind. I was simply offering my condolences."

He nodded and looked down at the typewriter. "She was a gentle soul, too good for this world," he said softly.

"It must have been difficult for her. A woman alone with a young son."

"She came from a good family, you know. She wasn't raised to live this kind of life. She worked, when she was able, cleaning offices in the evenings. It was the only job she could find." He swallowed heavily. "It all took a toll. Her death wasn't unexpected."

"Still, I would have thought you'd want to take some time off."

"I am fine. Thank you for your concern." His voice was tight as if he was barely keeping his emotions in check.

"I don't know how you can be fine," Charley said, hoping to exploit the weakness she thought she'd spotted. "You lose your mother a few days ago and then the man who was like a father to you was killed last night. How can anyone be fine with that?"

"Everyone grieves differently. I find solace in my work." His tone had become hard, all emotion gone.

Charley was taken aback by the sudden change in his demeanour at the mention of Carter's death. "Had you stayed close with Robin Carter?" she asked.

"Why all the personal questions, Mrs. Hall? I thought you were here about your brother and the sloop."

"I think it's all related, actually."

"You think the deaths of my mother and Robin are related to your brother and his accident?"

"I don't think it was an accident at all. Hasn't Sergeant Bronson spoken with you about what we discovered on the *Lady Stonebridge* yesterday?"

"The paint? Yeah, he told me. You obviously know nothing about sailing, Mrs. Hall. Red is a common paint colour used on buoys and markers. You'll find more than a few sailboats tagged with red from rubbing up against them."

"Carter had a red motorboat."

"Did he?" MacNamara shrugged his shoulders. "That's news to me."

He was lying. Suddenly, helping with a cover-up seemed inconsequential compared with the other possibility: perhaps MacNamara was more culpable in Beanish's murder than she'd originally thought.

Think Charley, think. What's really going on here?

"My parents were killed in what everyone said was a sailing accident," she said.

"Yes, I looked for an accident report after we found the sloop but couldn't find anything."

"The truth is, I'm not sure it was an accident, either."

"Like your brother? Again, Mrs. Hall—"

"Just hear me out, please." A scenario was beginning to form. She wished she had the time to work it all out before she divulged it, but that wasn't going to be possible. She'd start at what she thought was the beginning and proceed slowly, gauging his reaction and adjusting as she went along.

He shrugged and indicated she should proceed.

"My father was going to be president of the rowing club, but after his death, Robin Carter filled that role. Which was very convenient for him since he was stealing from the club and my father would have likely exposed him."

"That's quite an accusation," MacNamara interjected.

"It's well-documented. It's the reason he was forced to resign last week." She didn't know how long the embezzlement had been going on, but for her scenario to work, it had to go back to before her parents' deaths. "I think he was taking the money to help support you and your mother."

"And you're suggesting that to cover it up he was somehow involved in the accident that killed your parents? You're wasting your talents at the newspaper. You should be writing fiction."

"Bear with me. Things go along fine for years. He's not too greedy, doesn't take too much, so no one notices the missing money." She took a breath. "Then, let's see, a couple of things happen. Your mother gets ill and requires medical care, so he's forced to steal more money than he can convincingly cover for. At the same time, Frank Beanish has tracked down the boat—sorry *sloop*—that my parents died on and brings it back to Kingston. All of Robin Carter's chickens are coming home to roost, so to speak, and he panics."

"And he does what? Do you think he killed Frank Beanish?"

"I did. He hated Frank and my father, ever since he and your father lost the Ontario Cup to them."

"If you believe he held a grudge for thirty-four years over a rowing race you didn't know the man at all."

"No, I no longer think he did. Based on what I've learned about him in the last day or so, I believe he truly thought of himself as a good man, only doing what he needed to in order to honour his friend by helping you and your mother."

"It cost him his marriage," MacNamara said quietly.

"He must have loved you very much."

"So, if I'm following your little story, you no longer think he killed Beanish... Mrs. Hall, I don't understand the point of all this."

"I'm getting there. No, I don't believe Carter held a grudge all these years, but someone else did. Someone who thought they were helping Carter by killing Beanish, disposing of the sloop, and stealing the Ontario Cup to give to him."

"I'm on pins and needles."

"I think it was you."

"That's ludicrous," MacNamara said, rising. "I've heard enough, Mrs. Hall. If you persist in making these wild and unfounded accusations, I shall have no choice but to order your commitment to Rockwood Asylum."

"I'm not finished yet," Charley said, standing. "I haven't figured out the why, but I think you killed Robin Carter last night and then stole his red motorboat so it couldn't be connected to the attempt on Freddie's life—an attempt you made so you could get rid of the sloop once and for all."

The office door swung open. She whirled in surprise at the sight of Mark and Sergeant Bronson stepping into the room.

"I know why Carter was murdered," Mark said.

Before Charley could even fully process the arrival of the two men, Corporal MacNamara had rounded his desk, wrapped a steely arm around her shoulders and was pointing his pistol at her head.

"Stand down, Corporal," Bronson said.

"No. She's my ticket out of here. Get out of my way."

Slowly Mark and Bronson retreated through the door. Charley tried to lock her legs so he couldn't force her to move, but he was too powerful and managed to awkwardly drag her along with him.

"I'm not kidding, Mrs. Hall. I will kill you if you don't cooperate." His voice held no emotion and Charley felt an icy dread trickle through her limbs.

Her legs felt heavy, but she complied and allowed him to use her as a shield as he led her through the station. There were stunned expressions on the officers they passed. Their guns were drawn but there was nothing they could do to stop MacNamara without risking her life.

She'd done it this time. She could imagine Mark and Marillo chastising her for going after MacNamara without backup. But she was in a police station, for heaven's sake. Wasn't that supposed to be the epitome of safety?

Outside they approached one of the RCMP vehicles.

He opened the passenger door, used it to shield himself and motioned for her to get in.

"Look, you are out of there. Free. Just go. Leave me here."

He raised the gun menacingly. "Get in and slide yourself over to the driver's side."

"Are you kidding me? I don't even know how to drive."

"Who doesn't know how to drive these days?" he said.

"Me, that's who. I grew up with a chauffeur and I take a taxi when I need to go anywhere."

She could see confusion cloud his face and he hesitated. If she ducked into the car, would that give enough time for Bronson or one of the others to shoot him? Could she try to knock him off balance by trying to push the car door into him? She tensed, poised to act. There was no way she was going to let him take her away with him.

A whoosh of air disturbed the tense silence and then the sound of a dull thump. With a look of stunned surprise, MacNamara crumpled forward and his pistol flew from his hand. Standing where her kidnapper had been was Romeo Arcadi breathing heavily and clutching a baseball bat.

Bronson and three other officers swarmed MacNamara, who had staggered to his knees.

"I thought I told you that you could go," Charley said, unable to think of anything else to say at the moment.

"Yes, but then I'd only have to come all the way back when you finished, so I decided to wait."

"Thank you," Charley said finally. Better late than never.

"You are most welcome, Mrs. Hall." He turned to the officer who was holding out his hand to take the baseball bat from him. "Will I get that back?" he asked, reluctantly handing it over. "It's a genuine Louisville Slugger, used in game two of the '45 world series."

"How are you doing?" Mark sauntered over to her.

"Good, I think. How did you know to come here?"

"Well, I went to your home, hoping to have breakfast with you and your grandmother, but there was no one there. I assumed she'd gone to the hospital and you to the *Tribune*. Grace told me about your adventure through her archives last night and said you'd come here."

"Mrs. Hall, can you come into the station for a debrief?" Bronson said. "You, too, Spadina and ah...?"

"Arcadi. Romeo Arcadi, at your service, Officer."

Once inside, Arcadi was handed off to another officer while Bronson led Mark and Charley back into the room MacNamara had been using.

"We sometimes use this as an interrogation room," Bronson said. "We have it wired so we can listen in to what's going on, which is what Spadina, here, convinced us to do."

"You're welcome," Mark said, affecting a small bow.

"Yes, well, I admit, when you first told me your theory, I thought you were nuts, but..." He shrugged.

"You could tell something was off with him," Mark said.

"Yeah, ever since we discovered the sailboat, there was just..."

"Cop instincts," Mark said. "You've got good ones."

"So, I was right. He did kill Beanish," Charley said. "We have to get to the courthouse and stop Dan's trial!"

"Slow down, Tiger. The officers, here, have called Kingston PD and told them what we know so far. It *looks* like MacNamara probably killed Beanish, but there is going to have to be a thorough investigation. They'll execute a search warrant on his home and maybe we'll get lucky and they'll find the clothes he was wearing or something else that's incriminating. But for now, I think all they're going to do is get the Crown to ask the judge to put the trial on hold."

Charley tried to dampen down her disappointment. It was a start, at least.

"What about Carter? Why would MacNamara kill him? He was like a father to him. If the corporal killed Beanish, it was to protect Carter."

"When I was at the station last night, Adams let it slip that Carter was very nervous when he called them. Apparently, there were two telephone calls. The first was cut short when Carter, or someone else, abruptly hung up. Adams said, and Marillo subsequently confirmed, there was someone else in the room on that initial call—they could hear an angry male voice in the background but couldn't make out what was being said. Carter called back about thirty minutes later. He said he was afraid to go to the station and wanted the police to come to him."

"You think it was MacNamara he was arguing with? That he was trying to talk Carter out of going to the police? But I thought Marillo said Carter was calling about an old case."

"It was an old case, but I believe MacNamara was afraid it would be too easy for authorities to connect it to more recent events, specifically the Beanish murder."

"You sound like you know what he was going to say."

"I do. Carter was a meticulous man. MacNamara should have remembered that. Carter wrote out what he was going to say to the police, just in case. I was still at the station when the investigators returned with the letter."

"Carter was afraid MacNamara was going to kill him," Charley said softly. She couldn't imagine what it would be like to know someone you loved, who supposedly loved you, was planning to kill you. She shook off her horror. "What did the letter say?"

"Take a deep breath, Charley. This is going to be hard for you to hear." Mark waited until she complied and nodded for him to continue. "Carter confessed to following your parents to Cape Vincent. While they were socializing with their friends, he overtightened the rigging so the boat would be unresponsive. He assumed the mast would snap somewhere in Lake Ontario and they would simply 'disappear under the waves'."

She closed her eyes in a desperate attempt to stop the tears, but they came anyway. "It wasn't an accident," she sobbed.

Mark knelt beside her and wrapped his arms around her as she buried her head into his chest. "I am so sorry," he whispered against her hair.

He felt solid and secure and so, so wrong.

She pushed herself back, took a deep breath, and stood. "I need to get to the courthouse."

THERE WAS a round of applause from the police officers as an unshackled Dan Cannon walked from the cellblock to the front lobby of the police station. A horde of media were being held at bay on the steps outside the door.

"Does that guy ever stop campaigning?" Mark snapped.

"I hear he was their most popular prisoner," she said, grinning.

"Only because he's such a terrible card player. Word is, some of the cops are fixing to get him back in so they can pay for an upgrade to the break room. Heck, they're even talking of naming the lockup after him."

"Very funny." She was in too good a mood to allow his sniping to get to her.

Over the past twenty-four hours, the police had discovered enough evidence to arrest Riley MacNamara for the murder of both Frank Beanish and Robin Carter, as well as for the attempt on Freddie's life. The Crown had officially dropped its charges against Dan and his case was dismissed without prejudice.

Rose ran to Dan and embraced him fiercely. She'd aged over the past few weeks, Charley thought. Her skin was sallow, and her clothes seemed too loose. But perhaps most shocking was she'd allowed grey roots to appear in her perfectly coiffed blonde hair. It wasn't only Dan's arrest, Charley remembered. The Cannons' shipbuilding business was experiencing a postwar slump. Nevertheless, she hoped Dan's exoneration would help ease Rose's burden.

Over his mother's head, Dan winked at Charley. "I knew you could do it," he said, gently disentangling himself.

"Now, hold on there, Sport. It was a team effort," Mark said, wrapping an arm around Charley's shoulder.

Dan's expression darkened. "I didn't think you were much of a team player, Spadina. Isn't that why you got fired? Why you're no longer a real cop?"

He had come to within inches of Mark and Charley, and she was reminded of the last time they'd been this close to one another. It had only been Dan's shackles that had stopped the inevitable fist fight.

She slipped out from under Mark's arm and stood between the two of them. "Enough, both of you. You're behaving like children."

She glanced around the room. The police officers seemed to be enjoying the confrontation, but Rose... Her eyes darted between the two men and then turned toward Charley. A small "oooh" whooshed from her mouth. She could see it, too. Standing face-to-face, in confrontation, the similarities between Mark and Dan were strong—not so much their physical appearance, but their posture and their attitude.

Rose cocked her head to the side and Charley understood her silent question: *Does Dan know?*

She gave a small shake of her head: *No.*

It wouldn't be obvious to everyone. But for someone who knew Dan's true parentage—that Rose was not his birth mother—the recognition that Mark Spadina and Dan

Cannon were half-brothers wasn't a big leap. Until now, that had only been her and Mark.

"All right, out of here, all of you," Sergeant Kearn's voice boomed.

Rose recovered quickly and she took Dan's arm and ushered him toward the door. She looked back at Charley. "Will you join us for a celebration at the house? You, too Mr. Spadina, if you're able."

"Thank you, but no," Charley said. "I haven't been home in several days and I would really like a hot bath and a warm bed."

Fortunately, Mark also declined the invitation, citing a similar excuse.

After they'd left the RCMP detachment, she and Mark had spent most of the day at the Kingston Police station, and then rather than go home, she'd ended up at the *Trib* offices where managing editor John Sherman had cajoled her into helping Lester Pyne flesh out the details for a major story —*his* scoop—on MacNamara's arrest. She'd left in the wee hours of the morning to come back to the police station so she could be there when Dan was set free. She could hardly wait to hit the sack, but she was also curious to see the story Pyne had filed.

"Can I offer you a ride home, Mrs. Hall?" Mark said as they made their way through the City Hall building in order to exit on the opposite side of the police station and avoid the crush of reporters.

"You're just looking for a free breakfast," she said.

"Would that be so bad?"

She'd never completely trusted him, but something had changed in the last few days. Now she didn't feel safe with him, either.

Maybe she was just tired.

"I've got a ride," she said, pointing across the street to where Romeo Arcadi was leaning against his cab.

The drive home was a quiet one. The usually talkative cabbie seemed to sense that she needed time and space to reflect on what had transpired over the past few days. But that didn't stop him from constantly checking on her in the rear-view mirror.

"Mrs. Hall, a word, if you don't mind," Arcadi said in a low voice as he helped her out of his taxi. "Your grandmother told me about your ah... situation with your husband."

"My situation?" Charley said cautiously.

"Yes, that he is missing, considered dead."

She felt as if she'd been slapped across the face. "Not by me."

How could Gran share her most personal sorrow with a virtual stranger?

"Yes, well, I wanted to let you know that I have a son. A fine boy. Dominic. And I thought—"

"Thank you, Mr. Arcadi, but my grandmother misspoke. In future, please mind your own business, and I will ask her to do the same."

As soon as she'd said the words, she regretted her pique. Arcadi *had* just saved her life. Perhaps Bessie's conversation with Arcadi had been nothing but idle chit-chat to pass the time. How could she have known that he would take it upon himself to try to set Charley up with his son? If Gran knew, she'd likely be appalled.

"I'm sorry." She turned back to him and forced an apologetic smile. "I am very tired." Perhaps she could talk to Stan Martin, the sports editor, and get his recommendation for a baseball bat to replace the one the police had seized from Arcadi yesterday.

She stepped into the foyer, surprised there was no one there to greet her. "Hello?" she called out.

"We're in here," Freddie replied from the drawing room.

"Where's Irena?" she asked, noticing the mismatched teacups on the table along with a slapdash array of toast and jam.

"She gave her notice yesterday." Gran sighed.

"I made the tea," Freddie said proudly.

"I thought she was happy here," Charley said, picking up a piece of toast.

"She said she didn't feel comfortable working in a busybody household. It wasn't what she was accustomed to."

"And, it means I win our bet!" Freddie clapped his hands.

She scowled at her brother and then turned back to Bessie. "What did she mean by busybody household?"

"She said you started asking her all sorts of personal questions. About her husband. About her life back in Poland. About her sister." She shook her head. "Honestly, Charlotte, I thought I taught you better than that."

"I was only trying to show some interest in her as a person."

"Well, don't do it again. Good housekeepers are hard to find. And harder still to keep."

Damn you, Mark Spadina!

"Is that today's *Trib*?"

Freddie handed the newspaper to her. "You've had a busy few days."

"I thought you were supposed to be writing for the paper, not featured in it." Gran sounded annoyed. "I'll have a few things to say to Detective Spadina next time I see him."

"Frank Beanish's true killer is behind bars. That's all that matters." Charley stood, tucked the paper under her arm, and kissed Bessie on her way out of the room.

Propped up on her bed upstairs, Charley read through Lester Pyne's coverage. Despite all the background she'd given him, she was disappointed to see how superficial it was.

He had the facts correct but he'd missed the point. Pyne had tied everything—the murders, the embezzlement, all of it—back to the 1914 Ontario Cup, which had been stolen from Beanish and found in Carter's home.

But it was never about an old rowing rivalry. It was about a woman. A woman who had loved a man and bore his child. A woman who was abandoned by her government simply because she hadn't been married to the father when he'd died defending his country. A woman who was forsaken by her own family and ostracized by society for having a child out of wedlock.

If not for all that, Robin Carter would never have felt the need to embezzle from the rowing club and Charley's parents might still be alive; Frank Beanish would certainly still be alive. If not for all that, a young boy wouldn't have had to watch his mother risk her own mental and physical health to provide for him—wouldn't have felt the need to take matters into his own hands to protect what little he had.

Pyne couldn't appreciate the subtlety of how the threads knit together to create the shroud in which Alice MacNamara was buried. Pyne could never tell that story.

But she could.

Her fatigue forgotten, Charley sat down at her portable, red typewriter, inserted a clean sheet of paper and began to write.

Looking for your next Charley Hall Mystery?
When the city's nurses begin dying from a mysterious illness, Charley sees a pattern and suspects foul play. Trouble is, neither the doctors nor the police agree. With the clock ticking toward another deadline, Charley takes matters into her own hands and sets out to catch a killer—even if it means risking her own life to do it.

Does Charley have the prescription to prevent a murder? Find out in *A Diagnosis of Murder*. Keep reading for a sneak peek.

If you enjoyed *Rigged for Murder*, please consider leaving a review on the site of your favourite e-retailer or GoodReads so that others can find out about the Charley Hall historical mystery series.

Want more from Charley and her friends? Head over to my website and sign up for the *Gayle Gazette* to keep up-to-date on new releases, exclusive access to special features and giveaways. Plus, you'll get a free download of a solve-it-yourself *Bessie Stormont Whodunit*. Yup, Gran has some real detective skills, too.

HISTORICAL NOTES

While *Rigged for Murder* is fiction, there are some incidents in the story that are rooted in fact.

FREAK STORM ON DOMINION DAY

According to the *Kingston Whig-Standard* (July 2, 1948, p. 1), the city was, indeed, struck by a "freak cloudburst" on the afternoon of July 1st. "Miniature lakes formed within a couple of minutes in low-lying spots, cancelling one baseball game and the horse races at the fairgrounds." The storm was called freakish because it was confined to a small band near the waterfront and was over almost as quickly as it began. Members of the local RCMP patrol ship crew were called to aid "10 slightly-soaked would-be mariners caught out in small boats when heavy seas rolled down Lake Ontario and into the St. Lawrence River."

CANNON'S DASHED OLYMPIC ROWING DREAMS

Another story from the *Kingston Whig-Standard* (July 3, 1948, p. 11) caught my eye. Written by Al Vickery and distributed via Canadian Press, the article features a Winnipeg rower who was the subject of a widespread search after failing to return from the St. Catharines Olympic trials. Like the fictional Dan Cannon, the real Theo Dubois thought winning the singles event meant he'd qualified for the team, only to be told his time wasn't good enough. In frustration, he took off for Philadelphia where he hoped to prove himself by defeating the United States' top sculler. Unfortunately, he was too late to sign up for the meet.

SNEAK PEEK: A DIAGNOSIS OF MURDER

A CHARLEY HALL MYSTERY, BOOK 3

"Hall!"

Charley's head snapped up as Managing Editor John Sherman's demand for her attention reverberated around the newsroom.

Now what?

It was late on a Friday afternoon in August. She had finished editing the copy for the women's section of the weekend edition of the *Kingston Tribune* newspaper and was about to send it off to the typesetter.

Editing the women's pages wasn't Charley's ideal job, but it was all she had while she waited for Lester Pyne to mess up enough for Sherman to give her back her old position as city reporter. Sometimes she was lucky and she was able to work in a story of real significance, such as last month when she'd profiled an unwed mother who'd been forced into poverty because of government bureaucracy and the strict societal norms of her class. The result had been a cascade of events that had resulted in four deaths. This week's edition was more mundane. It included a look at the wives of the men vying to be leader of the federal Liberal party, a nurses' reunion, a fundraiser tea hosted by the Imperial Order Daughters of the Empire (*thanks, Gran*), and various engagement and wedding announcements.

Charley followed Sherman into his office. Lester Pyne was lounging comfortably on the couch, shrouded in a cloud of smoke from the Chesterfield-brand cigarette he held between his tobacco-stained fingers. She remained standing while Sherman circled his desk and sat down.

"What's up, boss?" she asked.

"Pyne, here, has heard some chatter on the police scanner. There's been an incident involving some of the nurses who are in town this week. I think you should check it out."

"Why me?" Charley swung around and glared at Pyne. She knew why. It was five-thirty on a Friday and Pyne could not wait to clock out.

"You were covering those nurses, weren't you?" Pyne said.

"I included a notice of their reunion, which was provided by them, but that's all," she said. "That's hardly what I'd call 'covering' them."

"Still, it's your story," Sherman insisted.

She blew out her impatience. "What is the incident?"

"A bunch were taken to emergency at Kingston General Hospital, that's all I heard," Pyne said. "Probably an excess of excitement. You know how women can be?"

An excess of excitement?

She ignored Pyne. He wasn't worth her trouble. But Sherman? He should know better. She rounded on her boss. "I do know how women can be and I doubt very much any excess of excitement warrants a trip to the hospital emergency."

"You know what I mean," Pyne said defensively, rising from the couch and approaching Sherman's desk.

"I have no idea what you mean," Charley said keeping her focus on Sherman.

"Look, Hall, be a pal and check it out, okay? It's probably nothing, but just in case it isn't, I don't want to be scooped." There was nothing John Sherman hated more than to see the *Trib*'s rival newspaper, *The Kingston Whig-Standard,* run a story he'd missed.

"Fine," she acquiesced. Her only plan for the evening was playing a few hands of cribbage with Gran, anyway. "But if it turns into something big, I get to keep it. *Capiche*?" She waited for the managing editor to accept her demand. He had a habit of passing her leads on to Pyne. She doubted this was going to amount to a reportable story but, as Sherman said, "just in case."

EXCESS OF EXCITEMENT.

The expression still gnawed at her as she pushed open the doors to the emergency room of KGH—Kingston General Hospital.

Ridiculous.

At the moment, she was suffering from an excess of irritation. So much so, she didn't even notice police constables Marillo and Adams as she stalked across the lobby toward the intake desk. It wasn't until she heard Marillo call her name that she paused and turned back to them.

"The nurse isn't going to give you anything," Adams, the younger officer, said.

"How do you know?" She found Adams' superior attitude difficult to take at the best of times. "You don't even know why I'm here."

"Probably the same reason as the other hack." Adams

pointed to a man Charley recognized as a reporter from the *Whig-Standard*.

Darn it!

"What can you tell me about what happened?" she asked.

Adams cocked his head to the side and allowed his gaze to roam the full five-foot-seven length of her. Charley bore his scrutiny without flinching. She had rebuffed his advances in the past. Today would be no different.

"Knock it off, kid." Constable Marillo swatted his partner's shoulder. "I think you could help us, Mrs. Hall, if you're willing."

"I'm always happy to help Kingston PD." She liked Marillo. He was a fair and decent cop who took the job, but not himself, seriously. It was too bad he had to be paired up with a pompous ass like Adams.

"The other nurses, the ones not admitted, are in a room through there." Marillo pointed at a swinging door where another uniformed police officer was stationed. "It would be helpful if you could speak with them, see if you can find out what happened."

"Won't they talk to you?"

"We tried, but they are terribly upset. The uniform seems to intimidate them. They're not in trouble or anything, but I can't make much sense out of what they've told me."

"Okay, I'll talk to them, but first, tell me what you do know. These are the nurses who were here for a reunion, correct? There are twelve of them."

"Yeah." He glanced down at his notepad and frowned. "I've only got nine. One arrived unconscious and three others were complaining of nausea and stomach pain. Five more are in that room, along with a chaperone. All we've got out of them, so far, is that they've been together—all of them—for the past two-and-a-half days."

"If that's the case, why would only four be afflicted?"

"And that is what we want you to help us figure out," Marillo said.

"It's possible the four weren't with the others *all* the time, and the other girls are covering for them," Adams interjected with a not-so-subtle suggestion of a more nefarious reason for their distress.

"I think they might feel more comfortable opening up to a woman," Marillo added, apparently supporting his partner's theory.

"And in return?" She would do it regardless, but it would be so much better if she could get a scoop out of it, too.

"In return, you get the satisfaction of knowing you are doing your civic duty by helping local law enforcement," Marillo said. "To be crystal clear, Mrs. Hall, nothing is on the record until we determine what happened to those girls."

Want to read more? Get *A Diagnosis of Murder,* book 3 in the Charley Hall Mystery series.

ACKNOWLEDGEMENTS

Writing is a solitary pursuit but publishing a book is not. I am forever grateful to two talented author/editors who are instrumental in bringing my stories to you.

Joanna D'Angelo, my friend and editor, who suggested I write a mystery series and brainstormed ideas with me during a long drive to Toronto and back—and then hounded me until I actually wrote it.

Carolyn Heald, a historian, archivist and talented writer in her own right, she is also—and truly fortunate for me—an excellent copy editor who is very familiar with the city of Kingston as well as proper grammar.

In addition, over the past year I have been supported by the great team at Best Page Forward, who have taught me so much about the self-publishing world.

Finally, I want to express my sincere appreciation to the members of the Ottawa Romance Writers, the Women's Fiction Writers Association, Crime Writers of Canada, and Sisters in Crime, who provide unconditional support and a safe space to ask questions in this strange world of fiction writing.

ABOUT BRENDA GAYLE

I've been a writer all my life but returned to my love of fiction after more than 20 years in the world of corporate communications—although some might argue there is plenty of opportunity for fiction-writing there, too. I have a Master's degree in journalism and an undergraduate degree in psychology. A fan of many genres, I find it hard to stay within the publishing industry's prescribed boxes. Whether it's historical mystery, romantic suspense, or women's fiction, my greatest joy is creating deeply emotional books with memorable characters and compelling stories.

Connect with me on my website at BrendaGayle.com
& sign up for *The Gayle Gazette,* my newsletter, to keep up-to-date on new releases, exclusive access to special features, giveaways, and all sorts of shenanigans. And don't forget, as a subscriber, you'll get a free download of a *Bessie Stormont Whodunit.*

Until next time...

ALSO BY BRENDA GAYLE

CHARLEY HALL MYSTERY SERIES

A Shot of Murder

Rigged for Murder

A Diagnosis of Murder

Odds on Murder

Murder in Abstract

Schooled in Murder

HEART'S DESIRE ROMANTIC SUSPENSE SERIES

The Hungry Heart

The Doubting Heart

The Forsaken Heart

Heart's Desire Romantic Suspense: The Complete Series

Made in the USA
Middletown, DE
14 January 2022